Biggs
the Pioneer Cat

By Leslie Grubb

For G. Pat

Biggs, the Pioneer Cat

Copyright © 2021 Leslie Grubb

All rights reserved.

Editor: Brooke Vitale
Illustrator: Michael Gattas
Cover Design: Pipedream Studios
Interior Design: Sandra Jurca

ISBN paperback: 978-0-9852216-1-4
ISBN EPUB: 978-0-9852216-2-1
LCCN# 2021909800

Publisher: LGPress, San Marcos, California
Contact: Leslie_Grubb@yahoo.com

www.LeslieGrubb.com

"Death, the fearful,
agonizing death of starvation,
literally stared us in the face."

—MOSES SCHALLENBERGER

Contents

CHAPTER ONE

New Girl

MS. GREEN gently laid her sparkly, polka-dotted ribbon flat in the middle crease of the social studies book and wrote SCHALLENBERGER on the white board. "Okay, fourth-graders, what do we know about Moses Schallenberger?"

Winnie looked around. The only thing *she* knew was that her new school's name was Schallenberger Elementary. And she only knew *that* because it was printed in big, bold white letters on the green sign in front of the school's office. Maybe that's why her new teacher was reading about Moses Schallenberger, the pioneer. How was she ever going to remember that name, let alone spell it for her inquiring grandparents.

Beside Winnie, a girl raised her hand. "He was eighteen years old and one of the first pioneers to make it through the Sierra Nevada mountains and find Lake Tahoe."

Another boy shouted, "He almost froze and starved to death, and he was all alone in a small log cabin built by him and two fellow pioneer friends who ended up leaving him behind."

A third girl in the front row sat erect and proudly hollered, "He was an emigrant, which means he left one location to move to another location, most likely for better economical, religious, political, or discriminatory freedoms. Are pioneers and emigrants the same?"

Winnie instantly knew that girl was the smartest in her new class.

"Excellent question, Molly, and yes they are similar because both decided to relocate. The brave pioneers were known for being the *first* to explore a new location. Most pioneers were coming from the East and Midwestern parts of America and migrating to the new western frontier for better opportunities."

Winnie heard the boy in front of her quietly sneer, "Show off, Molly!"

"That's enough, Charley," Ms. Green said. "Now, for homework tonight I would like you to finish the reading assignment, then draw a map showing the route that the Stevens-Townsend-Murphy Party took to get to Sutter's Fort."

A map! Winnie thought. She couldn't even draw a map from her old house to her new one, and that is only a twenty-minute drive. How was she going to figure out the rugged, treacherous route that took this pioneer party over seven months to travel?

"Why do we have to learn about this history junk? It's sooooo borrrrring, and all these people are dead! And how the heck do we know which way these pioneer people traveled?"

Winnie secretly thanked this boy for his question.

The teacher shrugged off the boring comment while applying her lip gloss and quickly added, "Charley, that's what your social studies book is for, there is a map reference showing their route on page 91 if needed."

Winnie let out a sigh of relief and mentally bookmarked page 91.

Ms. Green looked at the clock then happily added, "Oh my, it's time to pack up!"

Winnie timidly looked around her new class as her fellow students chatted and performed end of day "helper" jobs. She still couldn't believe that her parents had decided to move during the middle of her fourth-grade year. This class was so different from her old school. They had individual desks rather than circular tables, and the walls didn't connect to adjacent classrooms, which made her new classroom feel way too quiet and private. Other students kept sneaking peeks Winnie's way, which caused her cheeks to flush. She had never been the "new girl" before.

Winnie nervously focused back on her young and very slim teacher, who had a pretty smile and wore a tight black minidress with shiny high heels. Ms. Green was a stark contrast from her old pudgy teacher, Mrs. Beasley, whose daily uniform consisted of grey slacks, thick glasses perched on a permanent scowl, and a ruffled blouse covering her neck to wrist.

Her old school, Oakridge Elementary, was so much easier to remember and spell. But at least Ms. Green's reading assignment would provide her some historical facts about the person her school was named after.

Winnie thought about the few details Ms. Green shared with them earlier in the day. Moses Schallenberger was the younger brother of Elizabeth Townsend, who was married to Dr. John Townsend and part of the Stevens-Townsend-Murphy Party. The group had split up because of bad weather conditions and a treacherous climb, leaving Moses and two others behind. Moses had found himself caught in the ginormous snowstorm of winter 1844–1845 in the rugged Sierra Nevada mountain range, today located at Donner Lake in Truckee. He was responsible for guarding six covered wagons filled with valuables during the storm. The rest of the party maneuvered the five other wagons down the mountain to Fort Sutter, California, which is today located in the state capitol, Sacramento.

Winnie's grandparents lived in Sacramento, in a fancy, gated 55+ retirement community with strict visitation rules. For instance, Winnie could only swim in the community pool from 2–4 p.m. or play pool from 1–3 p.m.

Winnie couldn't imagine dusty wagons filled with rugged pioneers roaming the prestigious, well-manicured streets of her grandparent's community. They'd get kicked out immediately.

As she packed up, Winnie thought about the morning activity Ms. Green had assigned to the students. "Imagine you and two friends—just like Moses and his friends, Joseph and Allen—had to quickly build a log cabin in the snow," she said, handing out yarn balls, chalk, and rulers. "You have five minutes to construct Schallenberger's cabin measurements—twelve feet by fourteen feet—outside on the blacktop. The only requirements are four walls and a stone chimney for your winter's fire so you don't freeze to death. Any group who doesn't complete the cabin in the time frame will have perished, so work fast and efficiently."

Then Ms. Green had blown the whistle for the students to begin.

Ms. Green had paired Winnie with Charley, the boy in front of her, and the smart girl, Molly, who independently finished the measurements by herself in two minutes. Winnie and Charley just stood in the middle of the log cabin yarn border with their backs to one another.

One kid shouted, "This is like the size of my bedroom. Was this the size of their whole log cabin? Where's the bathroom? Kitchen? And most importantly, television?"

Ms. Green nodded, then began to dramatically describe Schallenberger's conditions as the students gathered around. "No windows, nor a door. Just a walk-in opening. No lights nor electricity, meaning no phones, computers, iPads, playstations, refrigerators, or televisions. No bed, stove, or chair. And freezing snow piling high outside for just over three months."

The fourth-graders unconsciously moaned at the sparse, horrific amenities.

"Good question, Michael," Ms. Green said. "And you will finish reading about that tonight. But the short answer is, the party members didn't have enough strength to get all the wagons over the rugged mountains, so most of the party took about half the wagons with them. Moses, Joseph, and Allen volunteered to remain behind with the other wagons. They thought they had the easier job. Little did they know."

"So Moses, Allen, and Joseph thought the men from the party were coming back to get them and the wagons once they finished getting the first set of wagons over the mountains?" Michael asked.

Ms. Green smiled. "They did. But their group had no way to get back."

Winnie thought about her move and how her family had gained space and amenities. Her new house even had a swimming pool. But she was isolated from her group of friends, just like Schallenberger. They had both moved to new locations in the month of November. Was she a modern day pioneer like Schallenberger, even if she'd only moved ten miles away from her old neighborhood?

It was kind of fun to think that way, even though Winnie was still furious with her parents for the relocation. Didn't they understand how difficult it was to change schools in the middle of the year, and especially at the age of nine!

The truth was, they had been so preoccupied with the new house that they hadn't even noticed Winnie's frustrations.

Ms. Green's voice disrupted Winnie's deep thoughts as she animatedly grabbed her purse, coat, and striped scarf and had the class recite the closing school respect pledge.

Winnie sat still and quiet. She didn't know the closing school respect pledge. Her old school sang a good-bye song instead.

Then she waited for row three to be dismissed. Last Friday at her old school, she had sat at table one.

When her row was called, Winnie grabbed her backpack and headed for the door. A girl in a red shirt and a matching red hair scarf came up to her and said, "I like your shoes and your name, Winnifred."

"Thank you, and you can call me Winnie," Winnie shyly responded, realizing it was the first time she had spoken the whole day.

Winnie's chest warmed as the girl smiled at her then skipped off. She hated her old-fashioned, deceased great-great-grandma's name, Winnifred. And she'd been so mad at her mom for making her dress up for her first day at her new school, with these ridiculous green and yellow platform shoes and denim dress. But if they both helped her make a friend, she'd pretend to like her name and wear the shoes again tomorrow.

She quietly waved to the back of the girl in red as she skipped off.

Time for Winnie to try and find her way to her new home.

CHAPTER TWO

Sold Sign

WINNIE walked out of her new classroom with her backpack strapped over her shoulders, trying to remember the directions her Mom had explained earlier that morning.

"Go through the school field, then turn right on Richland? Or was it left on Ruth Drive?" Winnie asked herself. She felt like she was having a brain freeze, like when she slurped an icee too fast, or like when you're taking a spelling test after you've been sick for a week and you can't quite remember all the exact letter positions you had memorized the week before. The street names were mixed up and confusing.

Winnie could only imagine how hard it had been for those emigrants from the Stevens-Townsend-Murphy Party with their wagons and animals trying to trek over the unexplored Sierra Nevada Mountains with no path ahead of them. Winnie wondered how they figured out which way to go. They were trail blazers. Their minds must have been extremely confused and uncertain, too, yet they were so brave to try.

Winnie timidly headed across the school field, passing by several groups of kids laughing and chatting, unconcerned with their whereabouts, unlike herself. She slipped through the gate, passed the middle pole to keep bikes from entering the school campus, then looked left and right.

Which way was her new home?

Her face burned like hot coals. Why hadn't her mom offered to pick her up the first day. Her work couldn't have been *that* important? Winnie rubbed her palms against her denim dress and squeezed her eyes shut, trying to remember if she had said left or right at the junction past the school fields.

She drifted back to those brave pioneers she had learned about in class. Was Moses Schallenberger anxious when his elected leader, Elisha Stevens, declared his route from the flat Nevada meadow junction up into the rigid mountainous region? Innocent Schallenberger was probably thinking, *Are you nuts, that's straight up cliffs!*

Winnie had watched some rock climbers scale a mountain face with ropes and anchor attachments last summer during a camping trip. She'd thought they were crazy. She couldn't imagine oxen, horses, and wagons maneuvering up those rocks and hanging from ropes.

At least the pioneers had been rewarded at the top of their mountain climb with the spectacular view of Lake Tahoe! Winnie loved Lake Tahoe. She and her family vacationed each summer at her other grandpa's cabin, right next to the lake. This grandpa, who she called G. Pat, was divorced from the grandma who lived in Sacramento. She had remarried a man named Paul, who she called G. Paul.

Winnie treasured her summer week at G. Pat's cabin next to the brilliant blue, crystal clear lake. She spent her days paddle-boarding, mini-golfing, and bike riding to Camp Richardson to indulge in huge double-decker ice cream cones. Then at night, they had family BBQs and stargazed down at the beach.

Winnie chuckled as she remembered one summer when her uncle foolishly forgot the leftover hamburger buns on the cabin patio before bed, only to be frightfully awoken in the middle of the night by a family of screeching raccoons. How had Schallenberger survived out there in the remote wilderness for three months without any modern-day accommodations and roaming nighttime critters? Winnie shivered at the idea.

Donner Lake was a little over an hour car drive from Lake Tahoe. Maybe G. Pat would take her next summer to see the Lake where Moses survived that 1844–45 blustery winter.

Startled by squeaking bike tires, Winnie snapped out of her daydream. Two boys on bikes sped past, shouting, "You live down that street."

Winnie gave a small wave and whispered, "Thank you," as they raced away. Her chest warmed as she watched them pedal away. She thought one of the boys may have been Michael from class, who had figured out why Schallenberger stayed alone on top of that snow-covered mountain during the yarn measuring cabin activity.

How did those boys figure out where I lived? Winnie wondered.

Approaching her house, she smiled. On the right side, a shiny real estate sign in neon blue and gold print said GRUBB GROUP REAL ESTATE/SOLD!

"Those boys were sharp detectives and found a big clue on my front lawn," Winnie snickered.

Her second encounter with students for the day. Winnie would gladly keep the neon sold sign up for another week if it would help her make friends.

As she approached her new red screen door, she heard Buttons, her pet beagle, howling wildly in the backyard. She quickly ran to see what the commotion was all about and found Buttons clawing at the base of the mulberry tree in the center of the backyard lawn. She squinted up, then frowned as a fluffy squirrel jumped branch to branch, teasing poor Buttons, who continued to frantically howl. The old apartment had only had a balcony, which meant no annoying squirrels to tempt Buttons.

Winnie wrapped her arms around her dog's neck and soothingly said, "Ah, Buttons, I know how you feel, girl. So many changes. It's going to be okay. We just have to be brave like Schallenberger. Come on. Let's go get your favorite snack, peanut butter crackers with a glass of chocolate milk."

At least that will be the same, Winnie thought as Buttons eagerly wagged her tail and followed into the kitchen.

But as she searched the unfamiliar cabinets for the peanut butter, Winnie found a note on the refrigerator.

Gone To The Store

Need Peanut Butter

—mom

"So my mom had enough time to go to the store, but not enough time to pick me up from school," Winnie said.

"Rats, Buttons. Looks like jelly on crackers today."

Buttons bowed her head with her tail between her legs.

When were things going to feel normal again?

CHAPTER THREE

Biggs the Cat

WINNIE wandered around the unpacked moving boxes in her new house as Buttons remained on guard for squirrels in the backyard. At least Winnie was old enough to walk home from school by herself, even if she needed a little direction from those two boys on bikes. Her younger sister, Carrie, had to stay at aftercare on her first day of kindergarten so Mom and Dad could work and continue unpacking. She wasn't old enough to entertain herself yet, unlike Winnie.

In truth, Winnie was a little jealous of Carrie. It was so easy to make friends when you were only five—unlike when you are older and more mature and have different styles and interests. Carrie probably had three new friends by now, if not more!

Winnie headed for her room. In the corner was a very small box labeled G.G.G. WINNIFRED'S HEIRLOOMS. The movers must have misplaced this one, because all of her boxes were labeled: WINNIE'S ROOM. Her parents were way too busy with the office and kitchen boxes to give any notice to her boxes.

"What is an heirloom, anyway?" Winnie asked Buttons.

She peeked inside the box and found a bunch of old, dusty stuff: a jewelry box with a miniature ballerina twirling around that played music; a smelly old cloth rag doll that had yarn for hair and buttons for eyes; a petite, vintage English floral tea cup and saucer; a few leather journals covered in old photos and newsprint; and a brilliant shiny, gold bracelet.

She took the bracelet out of the box and examined it more closely. It looked like real gold. Winnie adjusted the latch and dangled the bracelet around her wrist while admiring its glimmer from the sunlit window.

Curious, she dug around the bottom of the mysterious box to see what else was in there. The last remaining item was a silver-framed black-and-white photo of an eccentric old lady with wild hair wearing catlike glasses and grinning while holding a lemon meringue pie. Several cats were in the photo behind her.

This must be her deceased, great-great-grandma Winnifred, whom she was named after! What a crazy-looking old lady.

She grabbed one of the ratty old leather notebooks and opened it for more clues. Inside the cover, in perfect cursive, the title read, *Biggs the Pioneer Cat, By Winnifred Iris Wheaton.*

What a coincidence! She had just learned about pioneers that day, and now she'd found her great-great-grandma's small leather notebook filled with a handwritten story about a pioneer cat. She quickly examined the gold bracelet and wondered if it could actually be a gold cat collar if readjusted to the larger size.

Winnie turned the page.

*Well, behind every adventurous yet naive pioneer is a wise, resourceful, intuitive cat. And for this gullible Schallenberger pioneer, it was I, **Biggs Townsend.** Let me tell you the story about how I saved Moses*

Schallenberger from freezing and starving to death on that mountain next to Donner Lake, and how we were the true historical heroes, and how the Donners overshadowed us with their dramatic and tragic story just two years after our stay.

Winnie gasped, scanning her surroundings for ghostlike beings. What was going on? This dead great-great-grandma's story was about Schallenberger, who her new school was named after? Winnie's fingers and toes tingled. She sat down against a moving box. She cautiously opened the notebook again while squeezing the newfound bracelet.

It all began with Moses losing his parents to a horrific disease called Cholera. Back in those days, the water was so bad. I mean really bad, like it had contaminated stuff in it that made folks get really sick if they drank it and have really, really bad watery diarrhea, the kind where you poop your pants constantly and can't keep enough water in your body, so you die. What a way to die—from diarrhea!

Winnie perked up. Who is this pompous and vulgar cat, and how did her great-great-grandma come up with his character? Winnie would have to research this cholera fact.

Tragically, Moses lost both parents to this bad watery diarrhea thing at the young age of six. He had to go live with his older sister, Elizabeth, who was married to this really old guy, Dr. John Townsend, who was really a doctor but looked like he could be Moses's grandpa. Marrying an old grandpa guy didn't matter much back in the 1800s, especially since the average life expectancy was only thirty-five, and that was if you were lucky and made it through childhood without kicking the bucket.

This cat sure used the word *really* a lot, Winnie thought. And her mom and dad were both forty. *I guess that means they'd most likely be dead by now if they lived during the 1800s.*

This is where I, Biggs, the marvelous and intuitive cat, came into the picture. I was

Elizabeth's precious pet, her pride and joy in her dreary, dusty, laboring farm yet soon-to-be pioneer life.

Basically I had two, nonstrenuous duties to perform to keep my plush, pampered life with my tailored pillow and gold collar. 1) Scare the mice out of the house. 2) Purr and snuggle on Elizabeth's lap when she needed attention.

Maybe a few tail swishes too.

Quite frankly, Elizabeth couldn't live without me; I'd be gone two seconds and she'd holler and coo for me. Don't get me wrong, I loved all the petting and purring stuff, but sometimes a cat needs to be a cat and get into a little trouble with the cat gang, if you know what I mean.

Winnie studied the bracelet again. The story mentioned a gold cat collar.

Was Biggs around during Schallenberger's time, or was this cat her great-great-grandma's pet, just like Buttons is hers? Could great-great-grandma Winnifred have been alive during Schallenberger's time?

There were so many questions spinning in Winnie's brain.

Truth be told, Moses was my only nuisance. He constantly threw rocks at my rodent prey, shot off his pistol at my delicious afternoon ducks, and cut into my precious petting time with bedtime stories.

He even tried to pull my tail once, only to run to his sister crying with scratches all over his arm. Hey, I went light on him. But I made my point. Let's just say, Moses didn't try that trick again.

He definitely wasn't a top pick on my human list, nor was I a favorite for him, especially after that scratching episode. Moses fell under the "dumb dog fan" group, rather than the "sophisticated cat lover" category.

Okay, I do NOT like this cat! Winnie thought. Poor Moses had just lost his parents to cholera, and all the cat cared about was his plush life with his owner. Also, how did a six year old know how to shoot a gun. Those 1800s must have been wild times.

Sidenote: You might be wondering why I have the name Biggs, and yes, use your imagination: I'm ginormous for a cat. I have to admit, I have magnificent, long fur with brilliant grey streaks. And I have these pronounced ears that I can flatten to make myself look like an ominous owl on the hunt when necessary. Add my glaring emerald-green eyes, which were passed on from great-grandpa Tom, who was one fourth tiger, and that makes me a bad-a** CAT. I even have a tattoo on my stomach from my old battle days.

This cat sure had an exaggerated imagination. There weren't tattoos during the pioneer days. Were there? This must be a story Winnie's great-great-grandma had made up. It was just a coincidence about this Schallenberger character. Although, Winnie did have to admit, the gold cat collar was puzzling.

Winnie closed the leather notebook and rested it on her knees, "Who were you great-great-grandma Winnifred, and why did you write a story about the man my new school is named after? And what's the story with the gold cat collar in your heirloom box?"

Winnie looked back at the notebook. This *was* a story about Schallenberger. Maybe it could be useful in making friends at her new school. Winnie decided she'd secretly bring the old notebook to school tomorrow. Maybe she could even sneak wearing the bracelet.

CHAPTER FOUR

Lucy

WINNIE was a bit more familiar with her new school on her second day. She knew where her desk was; she recognized her new teacher's face at morning line-up; and she recognized the morning calendar schedule from her previous day. As Winnie unpacked her belongings, Ms. Green told the students to complete the morning warm up sheet, which was long division.

Thank goodness her old school was a few weeks ahead in math, so the problems were familiar. Winnie finished early and secretly looked around at her fellow classmates. Her teacher seemed to enjoy fourth-graders, but she definitely had a life outside of the classroom. She was constantly preoccupied with her phone, hair, lip gloss and polka-dots. The welcome sign and bulletin boards were covered in polka-dots, too.

The students at this school appeared to be pretty much like the students at her old school: a few loud mouths, a few super brainy, a few maniacally athletic, a few know-it-alls, a few super sweet, a few social activists, a few jokesters, a few rich, snotty, and whiny, and a few blended varieties.

The girl in red sat two desks ahead of Winnie, and was in rainbow attire today. This girl appeared to be more of a combination of the pack, kind of like Winnie—a little mixture of characteristics. It would be hard to pin her to just one of the social groups.

As Winnie contemplated where she was going to fit in with her new peers, the girl in red, but now rainbow, distraughtly held her mouth and heaved her shoulders up and down like an inchworm on the move. No one except for Winnie saw her pale, worried expression until it was too late. She threw up all over her desk. Chunks of pancake and sausage flew on the floor as kids frantically screamed, staring and pointing at the gross projectile mess. The girl had orangish/brownish puke all over her rainbow shirt and jeans, and a panicked look on her face.

Ms. Green immediately asked for a volunteer to escort the sick girl to the nurse, but no one would raise their hand. They all moaned with disgusting, grim expressions.

Winnie waited while the distressed Ms. Green plugged her nose and shouted a second time. Again, no one volunteered. Winnie reluctantly raised her hand, but the teacher didn't notice with all the classroom commotion.

"Quiet!" yelled Ms. Green a third time before gratefully acknowledging Winnie's hand in the air.

"Thank you, Winnifred. Lucy can show you where the nurse is located since you are the new student."

This girl's name was Lucy. Winnie filed it away.

Winnie quietly walked one step behind Lucy as she shuffled down the outside hallway toward the main office. Her rainbow scarf flopped to one side of her curly brown hair and was the only thing not covered in vomit. Lucy slowly stopped, then turned around and grabbed hold of Winnie's elbow for guidance, her eyes closed. The trouble was, Winnie had no clue where she was going.

With an unsuspected, jerky twist, Lucy turned then bent over and her queasy stomach released a second round in the bushes. This time it looked like mashed potato cereal and orange juice.

Winnie trembled, a miniscule chunk of bile rising in her own throat as she patted Lucy's back. Lucy wiped her mouth with the back of her hand, her other hand still gripping Winnie's arm for support.

Winnie nervously detected speckled throw-up on her arms. She desperately wanted to bolt for the bathroom to scrub her arms raw, but the girl began to moan and heave again.

Winnie hustled the girl along, wondering where this Nurse's Office *was*. She couldn't handle any more vomit. But she was so preoccupied with dragging Lucy to safety that she didn't pay attention to where she was going. Looking up, she found herself outside the school premises and across the street by a neighbor's flowering shrubs. She quickly turned around to view the green Schallenberger school sign on the other side of the road.

What had she done?

She had guided this poor sick girl straight out of school, across the street, and into the neighbor's yard without even noticing.

Why had her teacher trusted her to find the nurse's office when she was still the new girl? And who the heck had left the front gate wide open? Her old school had a black iron gate that closed after the morning bell rang. No way could she accidentally wander away there!

What a disaster. And this Lucy girl with the rainbow scarf looked green again.

Winnie positioned Lucy's head over the pretty, soon-to-be disgusting shrubs.

"How much breakfast did you eat this morning?" she asked.

"Sorry," Lucy whispered in between moans. Then she stopped and stared.

"What's that sticking out of your pocket? It looks like pure gold!"

Winnie self-consciously pushed the cat collar bracelet back in her sweater pocket.

Suddenly both girls' heads swiveled around to see a frantic lady jogging across the street towards them, her arm waving as she shouted their names.

Lucy turned and heaved in the shrubs.

Thank goodness! A responsible adult from the office was coming to the rescue. She must have been the one in charge of the gate and didn't want to get in trouble for forgetting to lock it, Winnie thought.

"Come along, you two. How'd you get across the street? You must be the new girl. Ms. Green called from class to inform me of Lucy's queasy stomach. You run back to class now, straight back where you came from, and I'll take care of Lucy. Oh, and dear, the bathroom is to the right if you'd like to wash up," the lady added, noticing Winnie's vomit-speckled arms.

Lucy faintly whispered, "Sorry about that. You can tell me about the gold bracelet later, when I'm feeling better, and thank you, Winnifred. You were the only one willing to help me."

The office lady gently peeled Lucy's lethargic body off Winnie's shoulder and led her to the door opposite the main office, which had white lettering: HEALTH CENTER.

Winnie frustratedly acknowledged that her old school's labeling was Nurse's Office. Hmmmm.

In the bathroom, she lathered both arms with tons of lemon-scented soap until they were splotchy and red. She looked in the mirror to inspect her freckles and short blonde hair for any other traces of puke. Winnie stared at her reflection and thought about what happened.

The girl in red, who was in rainbow today, was named Lucy. The Nurse's Office was now called the Health Center. The front-office lady was out of shape and sometimes forgetful, hence the school gate. And she needed to be more careful with her gold heirloom bracelet.

CHAPTER FIVE

Lucky Charm

A FEW students suspiciously spied Winnie's freshly scrubbed, blotchy red arms as she quietly maneuvered back to her seat. The janitor had already removed Lucy's chunks of vomit but hadn't eliminated the stinky smell yet. A lingering mixture of rotten milk and freshly sprayed Lysol floated around the room. Winnie had to fight back the urge to gag.

Poor Lucy. Throwing up at school was every student's worst nightmare, thought Winnie.

Ms. Green pinched her nose and pointed to the front door. "Fourth-graders, we need some fresh air. Grab a silent reading book for a fifteen-minute outdoor break."

Winnie grabbed *James and the Giant Peach* from her desk and stood up. Glancing down at her backpack, she thought about her great-great-grandmother's notebook tucked away inside. As discreetly as she could, Winnie pulled out the note-book and hid it under her other book.

Winnie was relieved to focus on something other than Lucy's throw-up, walking off campus experi-ence. She reassuringly removed the gold bracelet from her pocket and put it around her wrist.

Winnie had so many questions about her great-great-grandmother's pioneer cat story. But right now, the only way to get answers was to read.

Opening the small leather notebook, she noticed doodled pictures in the left margin of a fierce look-ing cat, covered wagons, and a young, strong lad, with a scraggly beard, holding a rifle.

It was May 1844 and there we all were: 26 men, 8 women, 16 children, 11 covered wagons, close to 100 oxen and cattle, some horses, a few dogs, and one cat—me, Biggs. (Moses was counted as a man since his birthday was November 9 and he'd be turning 18.) The whole lot of us were walking miles and miles to get to who knows where. California, Elizabeth said, the fertile and golden land of opportunity. Whatever that meant.

These crazy pioneers averaged fifteen miles a day in all sorts of weather and travel conditions. You name it, we experienced it: rushing rivers, dry deserts, vast prairies, angry warlike Sioux tribes, hungry howling wolves, kind and helpful Native Americans, long-bearded trappers, sleet, welcoming resting forts, warm sunshine, herds of bison, plentiful game, and lots and lots and lots of dust. This journey was an outdoor adventure, to say the least, and my fur was coated in dirt. By the time we were a few days in, I couldn't even see my brilliant grey streaks anymore.

Winnie thought about how far the pioneers traveled. Her mom was obsessed with getting 10,000 steps a day on her Fitbit, which was like 4-5 miles. She quickly calculated that those pioneers and oxen were averaging 30,000 Fitbit steps a day, along with hauling all their possessions. Of course, they could have made the trip faster on horseback, but they needed all the supplies in the covered wagons to set up their new home in this tantalizing, foreign West.

Winnie filed this fact away so she could impress her parents at dinner tonight. But then she thought,

How can I also ask Mom and Dad about great-great-grandma Winnifred and her pioneer story without getting in trouble for snooping through the heirloom box without asking?

Winnie decided she'd have to give that some more thought, and went back to the journal.

Of course, being the only cat—and the smallest creature on this journey—I had the privilege of riding in the second covered wagon with the delicate Elizabeth Townsend. The dogs weren't so pampered. They had to walk along with the horses, oxen, and wagons.

Although previous emigrants had made the journey to Oregon, our party decided to try a shortcut to California. (That's why we became the first party to trek through the Sierra Nevada mountains.) The trouble was, Captain Stevens hadn't planned on such

a brutally challenging mountain climb, and he soon realized he could only get half the wagons through at a time. It was decided that he and the party members would take what they could, and leave a few people behind to guard the rest. Moses and two others agreed to be the ones to stay back with the other wagons. They picked a spot by a mountaintop lake that they called Truckee Lake, after the Nevada desert Paiute chief scout, Truckee, who directed us to follow a river that would lead through the Sierra Nevada Mountain Range to California.

I bet you can guess what we named that river, too? The Truckee River.

Pioneers loved naming locations, especially if they found something left behind from a previous pioneer group. For example, Pipe Creek, Pistol Springs, and Hat Creek.

I bet you can guess what was left behind at each of those sites!

So, yeah, we named the lake Truckee Lake. (Of course, now it's called Donner Lake. Like they went through worse things than us? No way!)

Moses and his friends, Joseph and Allen, were the ones who built the log cabin with a stone chimney adjacent to the lake. The Donner Party came through two years after we did. True, they were stranded for a tragic winter during 1846–1847. And true, one of the weary traveling families, the Breen Family, even stayed in Moses's log cabin. Rumor has it that the Donner Party's devastating conditions were so brutally bleak that they reluctantly reduced themselves to cannibalism, which is eating your own species. Half the party starved or froze to death, while the other half supposedly ate the dead to stay alive.

Winnie covered her mouth. *Yuck!* Her new teacher hadn't included this fact in the Schallenberger summary.

Winnie had never heard of cannibalism before, and the thought was making her feel nauseated. She couldn't imagine eating one of her family members. She'd rather die.

She wondered if Ms. Green knew about this Donner Party and cannibalism stuff.

Don't get me wrong. I feel terrible for the Donner crew. But come on. Thanks to them, we were almost completely forgotten! At least our group kept the original Truckee River name. Plus we have the distinction of being the first to make it over the Sierra Nevada mountains to California in covered wagons.

We paved the trail.

Anyway, by the time we got to this mountaintop lake in November, we were in deep trouble. Winter was on its way, and there was no visible passage down the rugged, steep, and gigantic mountains.

It was crazy. We had already traveled 2,000 miles to get to this place. We were so close to our final destination, Fort Sutter. And we couldn't make it!

The pioneers were really anxious. They realized their timing was off by a good month with winter here.

It was decided that my precious Elizabeth and five others would set out on horseback to get down those blasted Sierra Nevada Mountains quickly and reach safety in the Sacramento valley. The rest of the men, women, children, and oxen used all their strength and might to get five of the wagons down the mountain range.

No offense. I'm sure it was tough-going. They had to physically lift and unload the wagons and supplies around big boulders. But we did not get the better end of the deal.

They left six wagons behind, at the mountaintop lake, with most of the valuables piled high.

Moses and his two friends, Joseph and Allen, immediately volunteered to stay back and guard the wagons. Those lazy boys figured it would be the easier job.

They thought they could relax, hunt, and sit around the campfire. Their mountaintop lake location was far away from the Native American tribes that might want their valuables, so being on watch guard seemed like a piece of cake.

The party leader, Elisha Stevens, promised to return for the three men, wagons, and valuables once they got the other wagons and people down the other side of the mountains and into the glorious

Sacramento valley and to their final destination, Sutter's Fort.

Dennis Martin, a skilled Canadian, was the most knowledgeable on snow conditions. He helped Elisha lead the majority down the mountain range and tried to prepare the boys for winter, but they didn't listen. They thought he was overexaggerating. How bad could a little snow really be?

Besides, Moses knew the men would come back. The emigrants desperately needed their things in the covered wagons— silks, spices, expensive fabrics, quilts, pots and pans, farming tools, and seeds—to sell in California. That was how they planned to get the money to help them buy land then plant and set up their farms.

Elizabeth was so distraught at leaving her little brother behind that she left me as a guardian.

I was the lucky charm.

If Elizabeth trusted leaving her precious cat, then nothing bad was going to happen to her brother.

Oh, if only that were true!

Winnie peeked at her fellow classmates, paired up and reading with friends. She wasn't stranded on top of a snow-covered mountain in a log cabin with a stone chimney, all alone and freezing, but she felt just as lonely as Schallenberger must have that winter.

When Ms. Green blew her whistle for the students to return to class, she quietly walked back alone. Hopefully Lucy would feel better soon, and Winnie could tell her about the cat story notebook and bracelet.

CHAPTER SIX

Delicacies

MS. GREEN held up three brown paper sacks with big numbers marked on each. "Okay, class, I need you to fold your paper into thirds and label each section 1, 2, and 3."

Charley blurted, "Hey are we doing something that matches those numbered brown bags?"

This time it was Molly's turn to sneer at Charley for his lack of connection. "Duh. Why else would she have numbered bags."

Ms. Green just ignored them. "What would you guess the pioneers ate on their long journey?" she asked. "Remember, they didn't have a ton of room inside the covered wagons."

Michael's hand shot up. "Canned beans and iron skillet cornbread? My grandpa watches the old westerns on TV, and that's what the cowboys are always eating."

Molly's hand went up, too. "The pioneers were trained botanists, people who specialize in the study of flora, which means they knew which plants were edible, poisonous, and medicinal along the trail. Did you know instead of going to the pharmacy to get medicine, they used special herbs to cure many ailments?"

"I think they stopped at McDonalds for chicken nuggets," shouted Charley. "Yum, that makes me hungry. Ms. Green, do you have chicken nuggets in one of those brown sacks?"

The class laughed, but curiously eyed the bags.

Ms. Green glared in his direction. "Very funny, Charley, but I don't think chicken nuggets or McDonald's were around in 1844. There *was* tons of free-roaming, wild game like buffalo, turkey, and deer for the pioneers to hunt along their way. They roasted their catch over campfires, then dried and stored the remaining meat, sort of how we make beef jerky. The dried meat kept them fed while they traveled, and until they could set up camp and hunt again."

"Now," she continued. "We are going to have a jerky taste test to see which one is the class's favorite. I have three different flavors in each brown sack: turkey, venison, and buffalo."

"What's venison, Ms. Green?" Charley asked.

"Deer, Charley," Molly firmly interjected.

"Ms. Green, is the buffalo the animal with the big fuzzy head and little ears kind of like my grandma Nettie?" smirked Charley.

Winnie smiled as Ms. Green disapprovingly nodded. She realized that her new teacher was academically creative, while Charley was stupidly entertaining.

After everyone sampled all three jerkies, they voted for their favorite. Surprisingly, the class selected the buffalo over the turkey and venison. Winnie had never tasted buffalo or venison before and was intrigued with the new experience.

Then the bell rang and the students were dismissed.

Winnie confidently found her way home—no more jitters after being lost yesterday. Skipping through the front screen door, she animatedly hollered to her mom. She had stuff to share: the puking and walking across the street event, the girl in red having a name (Lucy), the pioneer's Fitbit 30,000 daily-step average, and tasting buffalo and venison jerkies.

Fingering the gold cat collar, she decided she wasn't ready to share about that or the notebook yet, especially because she knew she shouldn't have taken them to school.

"Shush, Winnifred, I'm on a work call," her mom reprimanded as she gently closed the door.

Winnie shrugged her shoulders, crossed her arms, and stomped off. This had become the new normal with this move—her mom's preoccupation with her new job. That's why they moved in the first place. Her mom needed a home office to work remotely and wanted a school within walking distance so she could cut out morning and afternoon drop off and pick up and focus on her new job instead.

Winnie missed their small apartment with the community play structure and her mom's attention.

Maybe I just need some friends, Winnie thought. She wondered how Lucy was feeling.

Winnie made some peanut butter crackers and chocolate milk and went to the backyard to find Buttons patrolling the squirrels, oblivious to the treats. It was apparent her dog was also preoccu-pied and thrilled with the new backyard.

Storming back into the house alone, snacks in hand, Winnie dropped down next to the heirloom box and opened the notebook. At least dead great-great-grandma Winnifred and her silly cat Biggs would hang out with her a bit. She rubbed the gold bracelet around her wrist.

Those three young, careless pioneer boys had no concept of what was in store for them that threatening winter.

The snow wouldn't stop. It just kept falling and falling and falling. We became cold prisoners in that little log cabin cell without windows or a door for a long, brutal week. Thank goodness for the stone chimney keeping us warm, or else we'd have been frozen dinners for the howling wolves within days.

After the long, relentless week, Moses, Joseph, and Allen decided it was time to depart their "guarding the wagons" assignment and try to catch up with the rest of the party, especially since all the wild game disappeared with the snow.

Two half-starved cows, Betty Lou and Sally (may they rest in peace) were too weak to make the trek with the main party so were left behind with Moses, Joseph and Allen. When the snow came on, the boys sacrificed the cows, dried the meat, and used it as their sole food source.

Moses, Joseph, and Allen, indulgently ate all of Sally's dried beef that first snowbound week and packed half of Betty Lou for the trek to catch up with their main party.

They didn't have room to carry the remaining half of precious Betty Lou's beef jerky, so they left it behind at the campsite.

Not one of those blasted, selfish morons considered rescuing me, so I was left behind, too. Probably for the better, since those miserable hungry souls would have soon considered barbequing me for my feline flesh once they ran out of Betty Lou's beef jerky.

Hey, cat cuisine ain't too shabby.

Wow, Winnie thought. First Ms. Green's jerky activity and now this cat talking about dried beef. Another coincidence.

Those pioneers had the weirdest diet. The Donner Party dined on their own deceased, and now these three young pioneers considered eating a pet cat. Totally gross!!

Winnie would gladly die from starvation before eating Buttons. She looked out the window and watched Buttons patrolling for squirrels.

The three young lads tried to recall Dennis Martin's winter survival instructions about snowshoes. They haphazardly strung some reeds together from the supplies in the wagons, but the snow was so deep and the shoes were so poorly made that it piled up on those snowshoes twelve inches high. It was like lifting ten pound weights each time they took a step. I didn't know how they were going to make it down the steep snow covered mountain as I watched them depart, but off they went.

There I was, all alone for half the day, when who should reappear? Moses.

He collapsed against the tree stump the boys used as a chair and sobbed, his shoulders slumped and his head in his palms. He seemed completely defeated.

I tell you, the kid was making me want to cry. It was a bit much to watch. I jumped down from the top eave, thinking about how I could console this overwhelmed, sorrowful boy.

I had moved the remaining Betty Lou's dried meat supply into a corner in the log cabin, so I grabbed a piece of the beef jerky, rubbed against Moses's skinny, cramped leg, and began to purr.

I'd never seen anyone so happy to see a cat in my life!

He frantically bawled while hugging me against his chest and ravishly gnawing on the dried beef in between sobs.

He was an emotional mess. And the tale he told!

It seemed that within a few hours of their departure, Moses's legs were paralyzed from piercing cramps. He'd gloomily realized that he was slowing Joseph and Allen down and couldn't keep up with their stronger strides. Moses had to let his friends move on without him and return to the log cabin alone, once his pain lessened. It was the saddest and loneliest day of his life saying goodbye to his friends. He didn't know if he'd survive to see them again, and he'd forgotten he had left me back at the cabin.

"Biggs, you're still here, my lucky charm, my pet angel. I left you behind, but you stayed here for me. I will never neglect you again, cross my heart and hope to die. I'm a terrible person, and I'm so sorry for being mean to you and pulling your tail and chasing you out of the house when I was younger. You're the most amazing cat in the whole wide world, and you just brought me a ray of hope! I thought I was going to die. My spirits have been lifted and we are going to survive, all because of you, Biggs," Moses rambled on while stroking my back and chewing his jerky.

The massage was quite soothing, since I had pulled a muscle that morning preying on a squirrel.

Guess I turned Moses into a cat lover after all. No dog would survive out here, nor be able to catch any of these crafty squirrels like me.

After that, Moses couldn't stop talking. He was endlessly sharing his survival plans, which included the traps. Yes, the three fools had forgotten all about the traps packed in the covered wagons. They'd also forgotten they had cow hides and quilts packed in there, too.

With the winter weather, I had grown the thickest, finest fur coat, which made me look ten pounds heavier and kept me warmer. The pine tree trunks were excellent claw sharpeners, too which aided in my hunting skills.

Moses set up the traps by the lake and baited them with some of the cherished dried beef of Betty Lou.

We had half a cow's worth of beef jerky and it was the first week of December. Winter had just begun. We needed the trap to work.

The next day was a miracle.

Moses came stomping through the snow holding up a dead coyote. First try!

We roasted that scrawny specimen in the chimney fire while singing some camp songs and decorated the cabin with pinecones, holly, and mini fir wreaths. We were drunk on the excitement of tasting coyote after the week's worth of dried beef for breakfast, lunch, and dinner. We licked our lips then simultaneously bit into our coyote leg and . . .

Yuck!!

We maniacally gagged and spit out the vulgar chunks.

Coyote meat was terrible!

Worst meat I'd ever tasted. What bad bad luck. We were back to Betty Lou's dried beef jerky.

Moses strung the dead coyote behind the log cabin.

I, being a skilled hunter, snagged another plumb squirrel for our dinner. This was the hard work I was telling you about earlier. Mountain squirrels are way more cunning than field mice and rats back at home. I had to bring my A game to catch a few.

To show his appreciation, Moses made me a squirrel cap with the tail attached, to keep my head warm at night.

What a sight, a ginormous cat with a fuzzy squirrel cap!

I had to admit, Moses was growing on me.

After a few days of empty traps, Moses came shouting back from his routine check, holding a beautiful red tinted animal in his arms. It was a dead high sierra fox with brilliant coloring. Our stomachs timidly growled at the sight of a potential meal. We didn't celebrate this time, unsure what fox would taste like. We roasted then seasoned with salt from the supplies and cautiously took the tiniest bite, then waited for our stomachs' reactions, and . . .

Oh my, fox was delicious—a delicacy!

We jumped up and down with joy, broke out the camp songs once again, and relished our meal. Afterward, Moses made himself a fox cap with the tail attached to match my squirrel cap. Moses played the harmonica as we danced around with content bellies and warm fur hats. We were becoming quite the pair up on this mountain range, next to this icy lake, in the dead of winter.

Little did we know that a wolf—we decided to name him Walter—was just within our vicinity, prowling around for that same *fox. He had been tracking it for the past day and viciously growled when he smelled it roasting in our campsite. He sat a ways away, watching us devour it with revenge burning in his eyes.*

Fox was like a golden nugget in the dead of winter, and Walter wasn't going to let us steal another one of his treasures that easily.

Just then, Winnie's dad walked in her room. "Hey there, kiddo," he announced. "Dinnertime, and no fast food tonight. The kitchen is finally unpacked and functioning."

Winnie jolted up, hid the notebook behind her back and pushed her sweater sleeve over the gold bracelet.

"Hey, Dad. I'll be there in a minute," she said, placing the notebook and cat collar under her pillow. After all that talk of meat, she was praying for a vegetarian dinner!

Winnie decided that she would have been a terrible pioneer with that diet. Maybe she wouldn't bring up old great-great-grandma Winnifred to her parents quite yet. She kind of liked having her heirlooms and this story secretly all to herself.

CHAPTER SEVEN

Quarantined

IT HAD been a week since Lucy's throw-up incident, and she still hadn't returned to school. Winnie was beginning to worry that she may have moved away mid-year too.

And to make matters worse, no one else had tried to befriend her.

Winnie picked at her morning toast then reluctantly dragged her feet to school, not looking forward to another friendless day.

Of course, it wasn't like Winnie was helping out matters, either. She had temporarily lost her voice along with her social skills and felt paralyzed when called on to respond or participate in any form of interaction. Winnie had been alone and stuck in her head too long at her new school. She felt distant from the other students.

Then there were those awkward moments when Ms. Green would ask students to pair up for assignments and no one looked Winnie's way. The teacher had to pair her with another hopeless student who couldn't find a partner, either—usually Molly or Charley. At least Molly completely took over and did the whole assignment by herself, whereas Charley was clueless and had Winnie do all the work. She felt like a school zombie—zoned out and uncertain of her purpose.

Winnie had also lost her appetite at lunch; she just moved her food around in different positions until dismissed. It was like a dark minicloud was hovering over her head and following her wherever she went. She didn't have the energy to try and blow the cloud away.

After lunch dismissal, Winnie leaned against the school wall and pulled out the notebook, hoping that darn cat Biggs would bring some relief for her sorrowful state.

Moses gloomily tanked!

It had been over a week since the fox celebration and the snow was endlessly falling with no clear skies in sight. He stopped leaving the cabin and stayed hidden under the animal hides for hours. He would sit and stare at the bleak fire in the chimney, his only motivating chore to rekindle and put a tiny piece of firewood in the hearth so it didn't completely burn out.

I was becoming concerned. I'd purr my best melodies and rub against his back, but nothing.

I'd drop pieces of dried beef under his nose ... no response.

I even playfully nipped at his strangling dirty beard ... zilch! This kid was drowning in his deep dark, lonely mood.

It was like Moses had turned into a lethargic snow zombie in that sad log cabin.

Do I have psychic powers? Winnie wondered. Both Moses and I are struggling through gloomy zombie feelings!

Wait. Were zombies even around during the pioneer days or was her great-great-grandma's narrative cat Biggs exaggerating again?

Winnie pictured a hollowed-out, pale Moses, with a bad looking beard, dressed in old fashioned pioneer clothes and a fox hat, all alone in his cabin. At least she had classmates moving and socializing around her.

I hadn't survived this far on this blasted journey to perish before I got the chance to join Elizabeth again. I was determined not to die a frozen cat. A cat has nine lives, and I'd only used up two. I was getting down this mountain and back to my plush, tailored life, and that included Moses. I needed a plan to zap this kid out of his bad case of the blues. Think Biggs, think.

The lunch bell rang. Winnie shut the notebook and put it back in her backpack, then headed to class. She thought about Moses being all alone in the mountains, trapped in a very small cabin with walls of snow surrounding him.

How did he deal with his isolation and loneliness? Not too well, she assumed after reading the last entry. Thank goodness he had Biggs to keep him company and pull him out of his depression. Biggs made her think of Buttons. Thank goodness she had Buttons. He was her only friend at the moment, too.

Just then, Ms. Green's voice broke through her daydreaming. "Class I want to share with you that Lucy has the flu, and that is why she has been absent all week. She has to remain home another full week before her contagious stage is cleared. Aha, I just thought of a new vocabulary word. She's being **quarantined**: placed in isolation due to infectious disease," Ms. Green announced with a proud smile for her quick, off-topic, new vocabulary word. She wrote it on the whiteboard for us to copy in our fourth-grade vocabulary dictionaries. It was our first new word under the Q page.

"A letter will be sent home today to inform your parents, and I would like all of you to make her Get Well cards during social studies."

"What strand of flu was she diagnosed with? Influenza A or B?" Molly asked. "My high-school cousin, a few years back, earned a scholarship for a research study abroad trip to China, with his advanced chemistry class, yet all the students were exposed to the avian Bird Flu, stain H5N1, and had to be mandatory quarantined over in China for two weeks before being allowed to come back home to the U.S."

Leave it to good old Molly to expand on the new word quarantine and teach the teacher something new. *Does that girl research all day long?* thought Winnie.

Charley shouted out, "What's the bird flu? Did your cousin grow a beak or something? Hey is Lucy going to grow feathers and turn into a bird?"

A few of us chuckled.

"Quiet down, class. Lucy is just fine, but the flu is very contagious. It can spread through the air. That's why lots of people get their flu shots each year. Did any of you get a flu shot?" asked Ms. Green, and a few hands bolted up.

"Ms. Green, I got my flu shot and the needle was really big and my arm was sore for days," Michael shared.

Molly matter-of-factly interjected once again, "Scientifically, the best way to stop contiguous viruses is to wear a mask, keep six feet apart, and wash your hands with soap and warm water for at least twenty seconds."

Charley moaned at her smarty pants facts as Ms. Green thanked her once again for the knowledgeable input.

Winnie perked up from all this information. Lucy, the girl in red then rainbow, who liked her name and shoes, and let her guide her off campus and sprinkled little bits of vomit on her arm, and saw her gold cat collar bracelet, was still sick and being quarantined at home.

That's where she'd been!

She'd make her the best Get Well card in the whole class and . . . wait, suddenly Winnie had another idea to go along with the card.

She tiptoed up to the teacher's desk and nervously whispered, "Ms. Green, do you need someone to deliver the Get Well cards to Lucy's house this afternoon? If so, I can do it for you."

"Why, thank you, Winnie. That is quite kind and brave of you. Let me think. Yes, I believe Lucy lives a block away from your new house, so that would be great. Once all the cards are complete, I will put them in this bag and give you directions."

Ms. Green held up a beautiful sparkly polka-dotted gift bag.

She sure loved her polka dots.

Winnie's chest expanded as she smiled back at her teacher. She realized her heart had been numb the past week, and now felt energized and full of warmth once again.

Winnie had some untouched chocolate chip cookies in her lunch box; she'd wrap those with her card, too. She quickly began working on the Get Well card with lots of rainbow colors.

"Fourth-graders, I'm going to put on some pioneer folk songs for you to listen to as you make your cards. Singing and dancing around the campfire was a main source of entertainment for the traveling pioneers. They'd play fiddles and banjos while making up some of their own tunes or sing old melodies to pass the time and take their minds off the laborious and dangerous journey," shared Ms. Green.

Winnie unconsciously added, "And harmonicas."

"What was that you said, Winnie?" asked Ms. Green as all eyes stared at her. She visualized Biggs and Moses dancing and singing to Moses's harmonica and said a bit louder, "The pioneers also had harmonicas."

Ms. Green smiled. "Why thank you, Winnie, that is correct. The harmonica was the most common pioneer instrument, since it was small and easy to travel with. I forgot to include that instrument."

Molly shot Winnie a surprised look.

Winnie perked up as "She'll Be Coming Around the Mountain" cheerfully filled the room from Ms. Green's Bluetooth speaker.

Michael giddily chimed in, "Oh do you have the song 'Home on the Range' or 'Tumbling Tumbleweeds' on this playlist? My grandpa used to sing those to me when I was in kindergarten."

For once, Charley seriously asked, "Ms. Green, where do you find all this old stuff about the pioneers and fancy kinds of jerky?"

Winnie had wondered the same thing.

She smiled and responded, "Amazon."

I knew it, Winnie thought. *Mom and Dad say you can buy anything on that site.*

Winnie's melancholy mood drifted out the door with each upbeat verse of the pioneer camp song. She thought back to Moses. Biggs needed to bring him his harmonica to try to cheer him up with some folk songs.

"Class, when you're finished with your cards, find a partner and write your own contemporary camp song using a rhyming scheme similar to a sonnet like this one," Ms. Green instructed and wrote on the white board, ABAB CDCD.

Charley shouted out, "Why do we always have to turn something into a learning project. Can't we just listen to the music, Ms. Green?"

Molly critically chirped, "Charley, we are at school to learn and Ms. Green is demonstrating thematic integrative teaching, incorporating music into our social studies curriculum."

Ms. Green rubbed her temples as if she had a headache.

I hope I get paired up with Molly for this one, thought Winnie.

CHAPTER EIGHT

Walter the Wolf

WINNIE'S wish was granted. She was partnered with Molly for the camp song assignment. As predicted, Molly completed their assignment in record time, so both girls had extra time to read while the rest of the class finished their songs. Winnie reached for her heirloom notebook. She hoped Biggs would pull Moses out of his depression with the harmonica, especially since she was feeling so much better knowing Lucy would return to school soon.

Immediate action was needed to get Moses out of his mental and emotional dumps from being trapped on this snow covered mountain for over a month. I needed a plan. We were running out of Betty Lou's dried beef and the squirrels were catching onto my tree trapping tricks. We desperately needed another fox to lift both our spirits and stomachs. The count of strung dead coyotes behind the log cabin was up to seven, but we weren't that hopeless yet to endure another gut wrenching meal.

Pinned to the log cabin wall was Moses's makeshift calendar. It showed that it was December 24, Christmas Eve, even a better reason to catch a fox for dinner.

Winnie suddenly realized that this was her last week of school before winter break.

What am I going to do over the long break without friends? she worried. *I'd be cutting paper snowflakes to decorate the community play structure and indulging in hot chocolate with marshmallows and candy canes with my old apartment friends if I were back at my old home.*

And the long break was going to make Lucy's absence feel even longer.

Moses had been saving the last coffee grinds in the covered wagon for the entire month, just so he could have his only cup of Joe on Christmas. How nice if I included a little fox pastry to go along with the Christmas coffee treat.

Winnie couldn't imagine her parents going one morning without their coffee. They had an espresso machine with little fancy white cups, saucers, and miniature spoons. On weekends, her dad made Winnie a vanilla steamer in the same fancy cup to drink with them while they savored their cappuccinos. Winnie's favorite part was scooping up the sweet foam with her little silver spoon.

But Moses hadn't had coffee in over a month!

*I had my plan to get him out of bed.
    I gnawed off some of the last remains of the dried beef and carefully tied it in the trap down by the lake. See, all living creatures need water, so the lake was the best bet to catch a critter sniffing around while getting a drink. Then I set out to entice a fox.*

Cat meat is pretty darn tasty to those in the dog family, which includes foxes.

I went around spraying and scenting the trees and bushes within the area to try and attract some cat predators. Those dumb canines love sniffing cat pee.

Basically, I was the appealing bait, just like those juicy worms on hooks to lure fish, except I could escape with my feline swiftness, whereas those plumb worms were goners.

I leisurely strolled around while tagging my territory with my cat urine and noticed how peaceful the snow-packed pine trees were at dusk. A true Winter Wonderland!

Hey, I suddenly thought, I'll have Moses build a few snowmen to celebrate Christmas once he's out of his melancholy mood after his fox dinner and morning cup of coffee.

Sure enough, in the distance I detected a brilliant reddish orange pelt coming my way; like I said, very few canines can resist the delicacy of cat cuisine. Yet trailing about a half mile behind was a big, ugly grey pelt that belonged to that darn wolf, Walter.

I had crossed his path a few times while squirrel hunting and he definitely had a dislike for me. Oh, and if you were wondering, wolf is in the dog family, too.

This made my trapping a bit trickier. I gave a few loud cat meows to speed up the process and get those slow sniffers moving across the lake.

They were taking forever!

The canines can't compete with the superiority of the felines. I'm practically begging them to chase me, while they are clueless, manically sniffing everywhere to find me.

Finally, both the fox and Walter perked up to my cat calls and the chase was on. Wow I couldn't believe how fit I'd become with wilderness living and hunting. I was like a comic strip superpower cat dude with my speed and finesse.

"There weren't comic strip superheroes during the pioneer times, Biggs," Winnie whispered. She needed to investigate some facts about this peculiar great-great-grandma of hers with her parents once she confessed to opening up the heirloom box.

That darn Walter had a much longer leg stride than me and was gaining valuable footage. The fox, with her smaller legs, was left in the dust and hopefully would go sniff out the dried meat in the trap, but Walter, was revealing his sharp, pearly whites, a yardstick away. I broke into a light sweat.

Walter growled within my tail's distance. Saliva slung from his hungry mouth.

The chase was getting intense!

Think Biggs, think, and quick!

I needed my feline special superpowers: the leaps. I needed my cat leaps to shake this canine wolf off my track. I sped past the squirrel pine trees and headed straight for home sweet home, the mini log cabin, and jumped on the short tree trunk to use as a diving board spring and lifted myself up in the air. I flew across the sky to the roof of our cabin.

My feline leaps were a few inches too short and I was hanging onto the log cabin roof with only my front two paws. My claws were struggling with the slippery snowy eave. I slowly hung there while my nails tried to grip the wood. Walter was on his hind legs, licking his chops right underneath me, and trying to bat me down.

Think Biggs, think, and double speed!!

I was sweating profusely now. Suddenly, I realized zombie Moses was in the cabin. I gave the loudest, most wretched cat scream of my life, (the kind that makes hair stand straight up) to jar Moses out of his depression and back to the urgent, present moment reality.

"Get your butt out of bed!! I need your help Moses and NOW!!!" was my cat screech translation. This pierced Walter's ears and he began to viciously howl as my nails could no longer hold on and slipped off the roof. I fell to the ground.

Maybe this was the end, I wasn't going to make it through my nine cat lives or see my precious Elizabeth again.

Walter was staring at me with those beady green eyes, saliva dripping from those

gnarly sharp teeth as he crept toward me,
licking his lips.

He moved closer, snarling. I closed my
eyes and asked great-grandpa Tom who
was one fourth Tiger, for guidance in my last
moments and then . . .

Boom! A rifle shot in the air.

"Leave my cat alone or I'll shoot you,"
Moses demanded with the most deep,
authoritarian voice I'd ever heard from him.
I didn't think he was capable of projecting so
much from his scrawny malnourished body.
Walter twisted around and glared at the
skinny kid with the rifle, which gave me just
enough time to escape around the back of
the cabin.

Walter gnarled his teeth directly at
Moses. He wasn't leaving without something to eat, but Moses wasn't backing down,
either. He was getting reading to pull the
trigger just as I cat screeched once again.

They both abruptly turned toward the
back and saw me dragging one of the bigger,
frozen coyotes around to Walter, kind of like
a peace offering. Then I quickly jumped

back up onto the roof. This time, all four paws easily made it. Walter stared at me on the roof, then Moses with his rifle, and then the dead coyote lying in front of him, which was four times the meal I would have been. He looked at all three once more then punctured the dead coyote's neck with his teeth and began to drag his dinner back home.

Winnie sighed. She was relieved that Biggs survived.

She wondered why Moses didn't just shoot the wolf. Maybe he sensed that the wolf's loneliness was similar to his own and didn't want to cause more despair killing him.

I leaped into Moses's arms and purred profusely.

"Ahhh Biggs, what would I do without you? Sorry I've been so down. I can't let anything happen to you, I'm here to take care of you until we're rescued, and we will be rescued because you're my lucky charm, remember? I promise, no more long-facing it because I have you here with me, and

Elizabeth needs both of our safe returns to the group."

Thank goodness Moses's dark cloud was lifted and Walter the Wolf liked disgusting coyote meat, because that was a close one.

I definitely used up my fourth cat life with that escapade.

Winnie shut the notebook and looked at the gold cat collar. Could Biggs have really lived nine cat lives and been around during Moses's and her great-great-grandma's time? If a healthy cat lived one life for fifteen years, then nine years would be . . . Winnie penciled on a piece of scratch paper, 9 x 15 =135. Whoa . . . a cat with nine lives could be equivalent to 135 years!

She shook her head in disbelief.

CHAPTER NINE

Mr. Cox, the Cat Nabber

WINNIE contemplated Moses and Bigg's relationship. Moses saved Biggs from Walter the Wolf, yet indirectly Biggs saved Moses from dying of depression in that little log cabin.

Strange how relationships evolve. They hated each other in the beginning of the pioneer journey, yet now were fondly dependent on one another during their tragic 1844–1845 winter trapped on the snow-covered mountain together.

What a pair.

The school bell rang and Winnie eagerly anticipated getting Lucy's Get Well cards. Winnie recited parts of the school respect pledge, then waited for row three's dismissal. She lingered by her desk as the other students shuffled out the door and headed to the front whiteboard by Ms. Green.

"Ah, there you are, Winnie. Okay, here are the Get Well cards and here is a little map to Lucy's house. You go one block past Richland, then turn left onto Gardendale drive, then loop around back to Ruth Drive, which is your new street." Ms. Green hurriedly handed the polka-dotted bag to Winnie.

Wow! She was one of the fastest teachers to leave school. Ms. Green practically beat the students out the door. She grabbed her polka-dotted purse, gently nudged Winnie out the front classroom door, then locked it. Ms. Green was hustling halfway down the hall to the parking lot, back handedly waving, before Winnie could whisper a good-bye.

Winnie looked down at the map in her hand, then across the school field towards the backstreets home. She took a deep breath and proceeded en route. As she passed Richland, she began to study the new houses. Christmas decorations had gone up all around the neighborhood. She saw blow-up reindeer and Santas, and lots of decorative ornaments and lights hanging from roofs and trees. One house had a beautiful menorah in the front window for Hanukkah. She looked at her map again, Gardendale Drive was Lucy's street.

A sudden "Grrrrrrrrr" startled Winnie. A growling, ferocious German shepherd bolted across its front lawn and headed toward her.

Winnifred froze in fear. Her legs wouldn't move. She groaned and clenched her fist against her chest as the dog's barking grew closer.

Is this how Biggs felt when Walter the Wolf was chasing him? Except Biggs ran while Winnie remained paralyzed. She squeezed her eyes shut hoping this was a bad dream.

Within seconds, a boy frantically yelled and chased the fierce dog. "Duke get your butt back here, bad dog!" He grabbed the not-so-savage anymore dog by the collar.

"I'm so sorry, Winnie, Duke gets crazy at times. I'm Michael. I'm in your class."

Winnie unclenched her fists and waited for her heart rate to slow down. She looked at the boy and recognized him.

"You're looking for Lucy's house, right? To deliver the cards?" he asked, dragging a now-submissive, whimpering Duke across the front lawn and back into the house. "I'll show you where she lives."

Winnie smiled.

Michael shut his front door, then whispered and pointed to the house across the street. "See, Duke also goes a bit nuts because Mr. Cox lives over there and he is rumored to be the neighborhood cat nabber."

Winnie examined the neat white house with black shutters and sculptured, topiary plants.

Michael continued, "Duke is constantly chasing after the cats that roam his yard."

Winnie thought back to Walter the Wolf chasing Biggs.

"See, Mr. Cox has these precious Koi fish in his back pond. Supposedly his fish are worth thousands of dollars and the neighborhood cats love to try and catch them. He secretly sets out hidden cat traps in his backyard. But we don't know what he does with the cats when he catches them. When Larry's cat went missing, we tried investigating and climbed over his fence, but he had hidden cameras and we didn't want to be caught on film trespassing."

Winnie took a better look at the tidy white house before following Michael to Lucy's.

She wondered if Mr. Cox's cat traps were similar to Moses's traps down by the mountain lake. And what did Mr. Cox use as bait? Surely not beef jerky! Huh, that made her question why Biggs didn't catch fish in the lake like the cats did in Mr. Cox's pond? She presumed the lake was frozen from the snow.

Michael's voice broke through her thoughts. "One night when Larry slept over—he's the kid with black curly hair who was riding bikes with me the day you were lost—we spied down on Mr. Cox's koi pond from my upstairs bedroom window. He was reading books to his fish. Then he covered the pond with quilted tarps. He's obsessed with his fish! Plus, we had nine missing neighborhood cats this year. Larry thinks Mr. Cox barbecues the cats, minces the meat into small bite-sized pieces, and feeds them to his fish."

Michael's eyes were the size of silver dollars as he shared this disgusting information. Winnie gawked, yet intensely continued to listen to Michael's story.

He abruptly stopped and pointed. "Here we are. Lucy's house."

Winnie looked up at the yellow house with a red door.

"Listen, I'm going to split because I don't want to catch her germs, especially since she's quarni— something, you know that new word Ms. Green used today and we wrote in our dictionaries? Sorry again about Duke, he's really nice once you get to know him. See you at school tomorrow."

Michael bolted back to his house.

Winnie watched him and was stunned. He was like a gust of wind blowing in all directions, and she hadn't even said a word or heard the end of the cat nabber story! Still, that was more conversation than she'd had in over two weeks.

Winnie straightened her blouse, took a deep breath, and walked up to Lucy's front door. Just as she was about to ring the bell, Lucy swung the door wide open with a huge smile.

"Hi, Winnifred, what's in the polka-dotted bag? I bet it's from Ms. Green. She loves polka dots. I've been soooooo bored at home. Whatcha been doing at school? Did I hear Duke barking at Mr. Cox's house again? Do you know rumor has it that he is a cat nabber? Mom says I only have two more days of rest, then I can go back to school, but then it's winter break so I will have missed like a month of school before I get to go back to school, and that won't be until next year, haha get it, next year is after New Year's. Do you want to come in?"

Lucy was talking so fast Winnie felt dizzy.

"Hold on, young lady, no visitors yet," said Lucy's mom as she shut the screen door. "The last thing you want is to get this poor girl sick over the holidays."

Lucy turned to her mom and rambled, "This is the new girl with the green and yellow shoes and old fashioned name, who just moved in down the street where the sold sign was in the front lawn, and she's the one I threw up on while we walked outside of the school campus, Mom."

Winnie's cheeks flushed with this rapidly detailed introduction. She held out the polka-dotted bag full of Get Well cards without saying a word, then quickly walked back to the sidewalk, unsure what Lucy might say next to her mom.

"Thanks, Winnie. Sorry I couldn't invite you in. My mom said no because I'm still contagious, but I don't feel contagious. I'll be back real soon," she waved through the screen door. "Hey, are you wearing that real pretty gold bracelet I saw when I threw up on you? Remember you were going to tell me about it?"

Lucy's mom shut the door, but Winnie saw Lucy give another wave through the window.

Winnie waved back, letting her sweater slide down her arm to reveal the gold cat collar bracelet.

Lucy gawked and gave a thumbs up through the window.

Winnie smiled, then began to walk home. Suddenly, she realized she hadn't gotten a word in with Lucy, either.

She cautiously chose Mr. Cox's side of the street, still uncertain about Michael's crazy German shepherd, Duke, but she kept her eyes peeled for naive cats jumping the fence so she could shoo them away before they got caught in the traps.

Maybe she wasn't as invisible as she'd felt earlier. She had made some connections.

Winnie had two potential friends and some neighborhood gossip to share with her parents at dinner tonight. She also filed away: don't walk Buttons down Gardendale Street where Duke and Mr. Cox lived. Buttons had enough trouble with the backyard squirrels and didn't need a scary German shepherd or evil cat nabber causing more turmoil.

Besides, Buttons had already gotten a few complaints for the late night bawling.

Winnie smiled again.

It had been a good day.

She thought about Moses's isolation and telepathically sent him a message. *Hold on a little longer, you won't be lonely forever and friends will come your way real soon.*

CHAPTER TEN

Christmas Miracle

WINNIE skipped through the front door. "Mom! I'm home!" she hollered.

"Shhhh, Winnie, I'm in the middle of a work call," her mom whispered sternly, then turned and fake smiled into her computer screen. Her mom looked ridiculous. Her top half was business savvy, with a magenta blouse, pearls, and lipstick while her bottom half was couch potato—old sweatpants and flip flops.

The outfit summed up her mom's demeanor lately—preoccupied with her fancy new job and work responsibilities, and only half functioning as a mom.

Winnie knew the drill. She was in charge of getting her own snack and keeping herself busy until dinner.

Grabbing crackers and peanut butter, Winnie flopped on the couch. Winter break was in two days, and the only two acquaintances she'd even tried to befriend at her new school were Lucy and Michael. She knew where they lived, but she didn't quite have the confidence to knock on their doors over winter break.

It would be a long stretch without friends.

Standing, she grabbed the notebook out of her backpack and went to find Buttons in the backyard.

"Biggs, Biggs, it's a Christmas miracle! There's a brilliant red fox in the trap! It's a sign from above. We're going to survive this winter hardship and will be rescued soon!" Moses animatedly rambled, waking me up from a deep, dreamy slumber with visions of partying, dancing cats.

Winnie had almost forgotten about the fox. She's been so focused on Biggs almost being eaten by Walter the Wolf. The trapped fox made Winnie think about Mr. Cox's koi pond and hidden traps. Were Michael and Lucy right? Was Mr. Cox capturing cats? She hoped not. Somehow, she suspected the neighborhood cats weren't quite as wily as Biggs.

Sometimes I can't believe the stupidity of these humans. He really thought that darn fox accidentally wandered into our trap all by himself. Oh my, these humans assume that we animals are inferior to them; what nonsense, we are the superior species.

I baited that fox with my alluring pee and Betty Lou's delicious beef jerky. And did I get any credit? Nope. Not one bit!

Oh, well. At least Moses wasn't depressed anymore and sulking under the cow hides.

Moses proudly held up the dead fox, which was a beauty, while grinning ear to ear. You'd have thought he strategically trapped the poor thing all by himself.

"Biggs, it's Christmas Day and we are going to feast! Break out the harmonica, prepare the coffee grinds, poke the fire, and *hang the holly, we are celebrating!" Moses triumphantly chanted, dancing around. I decided to let him believe his "Christmas Miracle," especially since he was in such a grand mood, but we all know who really made it happen: me, Biggs, the pioneer cat.*

"Okay, Biggs, pipe down, you get all the credit," Winnie said, annoyed. That cat was really starting to grate on her. But she was glad that Biggs caught the fox.

Moses wanted to play his harmonica again. That was a good sign that he was out of his lonely depression.

Envisioning the mountaintop celebration reminded Winnie that she wanted to ask her dad if they could find the unpacked Christmas boxes in the garage and decorate their new house tonight. She also remembered great-grandma Jean, her dad's grandma, would be coming Christmas Day. She was great-great-grandma Winnifred's daughter. Maybe Winnie could ask her about the story, Schallenberger's connection, and the gold bracelet. But great-grandma Jean was ninety-five, and her memory wasn't too good, and she sometimes called

Winnie the wrong name or walked out of her room only wearing underwear. So she didn't know how much help she'd be.

Also, Winnie DID NOT want to grow old!

Filing away the idea of talking to great-grandma Jean, Winnie turned back to the journal.

We sang and purred some carols while building snowmen. Moses built a traditional snowman with rocks for eyes, mouth, and nose. No carrot or scarf could be found. I, on the other hand, made sure my big, tough-dude snow cat had sharp claws of razor thin twigs, long whiskers from nicely scented pine needles, and large piercing eyes made of oval shaped acorns. Not a bad job, I must say, and there was definitely a jovial yet peaceful mood floating around our forest lake.

A few brave owls who had weathered the winter hooted along with our harmonica melodies; squirrels peeked out from their tree dreys (those are nests built high up in the fork of tree branches); Mrs. Squirrel tossed a few winter reserved nuts down to us, probably because I had eased up on chasing her clan recently. A shy yet colossal moose even watched us cautiously from the shadows of the tall barky tree trunks. Our tiny forest haven had become a winter wonderland.

We devoured our fox dinner and savored every last drop of the aromatic bittersweet coffee around the campfire while singing carols.

I had to admit, my eyes glistened as I filed this humbling, heartfelt moment away in my memory. It was one of those moments, you'd like to bottle up and make it last forever. The feeling resembled the sparkly glitter dancing around in a snow globe.

Well. Moses and I had our winter wonderland, snow-globe memory moment together on top of the Sierra Nevada Mountains near a deserted lake, next to a very small makeshift log cabin with no windows and no door, miles and miles away from another human being, and with tons of incessant snow landscaping our whole neighborhood.

I thought back to that six-year-old brat on the Missouri farm, chasing my mouse *prey, chucking rocks at me, and stealing my Elizabeth petting time. The eighteen-year-old playing his harmonica and endearingly smiling my way had come a long way. I wiped my eyes with a paw and purred back at him.*

Now that's what I call a real Christmas miracle.

Winnie peacefully sighed and patted Buttons on the head. Buttons affectionately wagged her tail and licked the peanut butter off Winnie's cheek.

CHAPTER ELEVEN

Gigi

FOR THE first few days of winter break, Winnie kept herself busy putting up Christmas decorations. G. Pat was due over any minute, and he was bringing great-grandma Jean, whose nickname was Gigi for the two g's in great-grandma.

Winnie was hoping to find some private time with Gigi. Detective work was needed to get answers regarding the notebook story, Biggs, Schallenberger, and the cat collar bracelet. She desperately hoped that her Gigi's memory was working today. She wanted to know why her great-great-grandma Winnifred had written the pioneer story.

Winnie recognized upbeat humming coming from the front door. Gigi loved humming tunes.

"Hi, squirt! How's the new pad and the new school and where's that crazy beagle of yours?" G. Pat bellowed as he picked her up and flung her in the air. Buttons heard the new voices and quickly came to inspect. She ran in circles around G. Pat.

"Gigi, let's get you over here in the comfy chair. Don't you look nice in your holiday outfit," her mom said, gently guiding the old lady to the cushioned seat in the corner of the living room.

Winnie noticed Gigi had chalklike penciled half circles drawn as eyebrows. She resembled a turtle in her dark green velvet sweatsuit, robust middle, and crew cut hair style.

"Well, who is this young lady? I recognize you from the old neighborhood. Do you still have that white pony with the sparkly saddle in your backyard?" Gigi asked, bending down to stare absently into Winnie's eyes. She saw lots of gold fillings in the old lady's smile.

"Gigi, this is Winnifred, named after your mom. Remember, she's in the fourth-grade now?" Winnie's mom explained.

"Oh, now I remember you, darling. You liked that crazy Schallenberger kid down the street who gave you that ginormous stuffed cat he won at the State Fair. I never liked that stuffed cat. Too pompous looking," Gigi triumphantly recalled.

Winnie realized she was referring to her mom, great-great-grandma Winnifred. Maybe Moses had won her a stuffed animal Biggs!

Winnie was more sure than ever now that the answers to her questions lay somewhere in Gigi's confused brain. Maybe her great-great-grandma wrote the story because her high school sweetheart was related to Moses Schallenberger?

"Gigi, was the ginormous stuffed cat named Biggs? And did your mom know Moses Schallenberger?" she excitedly asked.

G. Pat interjected, "Silly Gigi, this is your great-granddaughter Winnie, not your mother. And she has a pet dog named Buttons, not a big stuffed cat or white pony. Did you take all your medication this morning?" He patted her back, then asked Winnie to get her a candy cane cookie. "Let's get a little sugar in that brain of yours to wake it up."

Winnie remained still, staring in disbelief, then continued asking, "Gigi, did great-great-grandma

Winnifred write a story about pioneer Moses and that cat?"

Her mom snapped, "Winnie, what's gotten into you? You're talking nonsense now. You heard your grandpa, go get Gigi a cookie and some eggnog."

Something was stored away in this Gigi's memory about the notebook and story, Winnie could feel it in her bones; her comments weren't just a coincidence. She ran to her room and grabbed the gold cat collar bracelet and old black-and-white picture, then headed to the kitchen to get the candy cane cookie and eggnog.

Winnie cautiously waited with her back against the kitchen wall for the room to clear out of relatives, then beelined for Gigi, who was peacefully humming in the chair.

She handed her the treats then whispered, "Gigi, can you tell me more about your mom and pioneer Schallenberger? Did he have a real cat named Biggs or was it just a stuffed animal from the fair?"

"Oh, what delicious cookies. Did you help make these dear?" Gigi hummed. "I don't get these special treats at the dining hall. They keep us on a strict diet. But I do play bingo on Tuesdays—or is it Thursdays?"

Winnie needed to think fast. She knew she wouldn't get many opportunities alone with her great-grandma. She held up her wrist and let the brilliant gold bracelet flash in front of her.

Gigi's face immediately lit up with recognition and delight. "Oh, you found it! I secretly tucked that away for you in a little box right before I had to move out of my house and into that darn old people's home. I don't know why I had to move, I don't feel that old."

She continued, "You were named after my mom, did you know that? So I thought you deserved the special treasured heirlooms from her. Do you know I had a beautiful rose garden in my old house?" She sipped some more eggnog.

Winnie felt pins and needles igniting her whole body. "Gigi, how did you get this bracelet?"

"Oh it's a long folktale story, goes back generations, back to the gold rush actually. That's why it's an heirloom, honey, but it was originally a cat collar. Your great-great-grandma Winifred turned it into a bracelet when it was passed on to her. She was obsessed with cats, did you know that? She had, like, nine at one point. She turned it back into a cat collar for one of her special felines. I guess it really can be used as both."

Gigi rambled, "Do you know one of the great grandkids is named after my mom? I think it's Uncle Nick's son. I don't get sugar cookies with icing back at the old folk's home, only tapioca pudding which is lumpy."

Winnie was so confused by Gigi's nonsense babbling. She looked at the old lady's stomach, which resembled a big bowl of tapioca pudding, and thought she might be better off sticking to cookies.

Winnie was losing her great-grandma's attention again. She suggested another sip of eggnog to her very old great grandma.

"So, Gigi, you gave me the heirloom box from your mom? But how did your mom get the cat collar bracelet in the first place? Please, try and remember, it's really important," Winnie pleaded.

"Hmmmmmm It was from her high school sweetheart, who was named after his great-great-grandpa Moses. He was some type of pioneer hero who survived a whole winter's snowstorm up in the Sierra Nevada mountain range a few years before the gold rush. The great-great-grandpa Moses was honored with the gold nugget for his feats, and he turned it into a cat collar for his foolish cat, whom he superstitiously thought was a lucky charm. It was eventually passed down to the great-great-grandson who was named after him, just like the heirloom box was passed on to you. He was madly in love with your great-great-grandma Winnifred, so he gave it to her."

"Cathy, pass me my purse please," Gigi said, and began to smear bright red lipstick all over her face.

I really really don't want to grow old, thought Winnie, *and why did she just call me Cathy? That's my mom's name.*

This was good information, though. The puzzle pieces were slowly fitting together. Maybe Biggs was a real cat, after all.

"Whoa, slow down there Gigi, it's Christmas, not Halloween," G. Pat said as he reappeared, then wiped the smeared lipstick off her face. "Let's have you look at this instead."

He placed a magazine in her hands and she drifted off humming once again.

"Run along now, Winnie. I'll sit with her for a bit. She'll be dozing off in no time. Sorry about the mixed-up names. Her memory goes often now, but she loves you very much when she's healthy and coherent," chimed G. Pat.

Gigi's eyelids began to droop, so Winnie headed for the dining room with the rest of the other relatives. Her brain was spinning from the clues Gigi had given her.

"You forgot this, squirt," G. Pat said, handing her the black-and-white picture frame. Then he stopped and examined it more closely. "Hey this is your great-great-grandma Winnifred. She was such an eccentric old bird. Made the best lemon meringue pies, obsessively wrote stories all the time, and had a slew of eclectic cats. I never knew her without a cat or a notebook around. Hey, look, over here in the background of this picture, hidden in the corner. That was her favorite cat. He was a mean one. Scratched me once when I was a kid," he pointed to the bottom of the old black-and-white photo. Sure enough, in the shadows, sat a ginormous, glaring and grinning cat with a hint of gold around his furry grey neck.

How had Winnie missed this? She guessed she was too focused on the catlike glasses and lemon meringue pie in the picture

Was that Biggs? Her great-great-grandma's book character?

Or was Biggs really Schallenberger's pet cat?

Was it even remotely possible that Biggs really had lived nine lives, and had lived during both time periods?

Winnie felt dizzy with all the parallels. She definitely ruled out the stuffed animal state fair cat, though, since she'd learned about two real cats.

She thought about the other things she'd learned today:

Her great-great-grandma Winnifred loved cats, writing stories, baking lemon meringue pies, and more importantly maybe had a sweetheart that was the great-great-grandson to Moses Schallenberger. Oh, and she may have received the gold cat collar bracelet as a gift, which was an heirloom passed down from the original Moses to his great-great-grandson.

She also knew that great-great-grandma Winnifred had used the gold bracelet as a cat collar for her favorite cat, who looked like Biggs in her story. And that the ancient heirloom gold collar had been passed on to her by Gigi. She was getting a headache trying to timeline the gold cat collar bracelet. She looked down at the gold bracelet in awe.

How old are you? She wondered.

The Gold Rush was in 1849, four years after Moses and Bigg's rescue. She easily recalled this date because her dad's favorite football team, the forty-niners, was named after the year of the gold rush in 1849.

Was everything named after history?

She got a piece of scratch paper and wrote down the current year, then subtracted the gold rush year 1849 which equated to just over 170 years. Her heirloom bracelet was possibly 170 years old!

She mulled this new information while snacking on a candy cane cookie and thought how clever her great-great-grandma was in writing about this historical event.

Gigi was fast asleep in the corner chair quietly snoring.

CHAPTER TWELVE

January Literature

POST-CHRISTMAS melancholy quickly set in, especially with the current cold weather conditions. Gifts had been exchanged, family had come and gone, decorations were boxed away for next year, and the rain continued to pitter-patter. At least it wasn't bone-chilling temperatures and piled up snow like Moses and Biggs's situation. They had been bored stiff after their Christmas fox dinner and idly sat in their lonely log cabin watching the snowflakes fall.

Winnie had chickened out of going to Lucy or Michael's house unannounced, so was lonely and bored over her winter break, too. She desperately hoped Lucy was as excited to see her as she was to see Lucy when school started again.

Winnie hadn't gotten any more answers out of her elderly and confused Gigi, so she decided to ask Ms. Green a few more details about Moses Schallenberger and his winter ordeal to fact-check her great-great-grandma Winnifred's story.

Examining the old leather notebook, she realized her bookmark was close to the end. She flipped through the book and saw that she only had two chapters left.

"Biggs, Biggs, look what I found in one of the covered wagons," shouted Moses from across the snow-packed yard.

It better be something tasty, because I was getting really sick of nuts, fox, pine needles, nuts, squirrel, pine needles, nuts, nuts, and nuts food sources. We had finished the old dried beef weeks ago.

I slowly responded with a suspicious glare in Moses's direction. He walked toward me, revealing an armful of thick paper bound rectangles.

Those aren't edible, you fool!

"Biggs, I found Dr. Townsend's books. We have something to entertain us besides dreaming about food and warm places," Moses informed me. "This one here is the Bible, with lots of stories about people and morals, and this one here is Lord Chesterfield's letters to his son about how to behave in a polite society, and this one is Lord Byron's Poems with many descriptions about nature, storms, and love. What luck, Biggs!" Moses rejoiced as he picked me up and swung me around in circles.

What was he so happy about? I nibbled on the end of one of these so-called books and instantly spit it out. It had no flavor whatsoever. Even salt and pepper wouldn't have helped with the blandness.

We needed food and wood for the fire for our survival, not tidy, well-bound cardboard.

We were freezing and wasting away.

He must have been hallucinating from hunger if he thought those books were of any use, unless he contemplated using them as kindling, but we still had a pile of wood outside our log cabin.

Moses heated some snow with bits of pine needle in the kettle for flavor, then threw a pine knot on the fire. We'd learned while experimenting with alternative food choices earlier in the week that these handy dandy pine knots were terrible tasting but created a bright, glowing night light.

Moses plucked me on his lap and began to read one of Lord Byron's poems with mugs of hot-flavored snow tea in hand:

She walks in beauty, like the night
Of cloudless climes and starry skies;
And all that's best of dark and bright
Meet in her aspect and her eyes;

Yowza! Now we're talking! My ears perked up to this magic melody of words.

How romantic and calming to the heart! His words made me forget about my rumbling stomach. Moses's reading voice was like a soft lullaby. I hazily drifted back to my younger years, visualizing Tricksy, my first cat love, with her brilliant blue eyes fluttering up at me on our midnight cat prowls as I'd go in for the smooch. I hadn't thought of her in ages and relished the fond memories. I purred and purred, encouraging Moses to continue with the poem. He had a serene, distant look on his face, too, like he was recalling a past crush. Then again, he was so young that maybe he was fantasizing about a future love. Who knows with these two-legged creatures.

Moses continued alright, night after night after night for that whole, long, dreary month of January. We learned to sleep in as late as possible so our cold snowy days would be short, then stock up on the pine knots, snow tea, and quilts for our late nights of faraway stories and imaginary characters that tenderly carried us through the hardest part of winter. I actually don't know if we would have survived without our January literature to take our minds off our terrible situation.

Then, late into the month, we stumbled across the book **Robinson Crusoe**. The character in this novel was a stranded, relatable, fellow companion. Young Robinson was a crazy and impulsive English boy who *ditched his parent's wishes of caution and calculation for adventure on a wretched ship. Unfortunately, he wasn't the best at sea, and was shipwrecked for twenty-eight years on a remote island.*

Talk about learning survival skills! We clearly related to Robinson's constant obsession with food and survival. And he didn't have a cat to rescue him, I gently clawed Moses on the arm as a friendly reminder of my purposeful presence.

Winnie realized she had never had to think about her food sources the way Schallenberger and now this Robinson Crusoe kid had. All she did was open the cabinet or refrigerator and see what options she had to choose from. And if something was missing, it went on the grocery store list for the next visit.

I guess I'm luckier than I realized, she thought.

"Stop that Biggs!" Moses said, clearly not liking my clawing. He shut the book, rubbed his arm, and looked at our etched log calendar. He couldn't believe his eyes when

he scratched off another day on the log wall;
we'd been stranded for over two months now.

Moses whispered nervously, "Biggs, it
can't be much longer, can it? Tomorrow is
February first. Someone will come soon to
rescue us, right? I mean, they know where
they left us, and we have all the wagons—
unlike Robinson Crusoe, who was stranded
on a desolate island unknown to anyone."

Okay now I felt bad for scratching this
kid. His voice was full of panic.

I think the twenty-eight years of the
Robinson Crusoe's isolation story was
giving Moses some doubts about our rescue.
I watched him shake, rubbing his leg with
my furry neck. Then I jumped on Lord
Byron's poetry book, which we had read
at the beginning of the month; I needed
to distract this kid with the light-hearted,
dreamy, romance stuff again. A little more
hopeful words about future loves and dating.

He smiled and grabbed the poems, "Ahh,
you like the romance better, Biggs. Good
idea. Maybe we will finish Robinson Crusoe
another time, once we have been rescued and

are back to civilization. That story is too close to reality at the moment."

My stomach ached from hunger pains. We hadn't trapped a fox in a few days. But I jumped on his lap, settling in for another long, tea sipping, snowy night. I was too tired to hunt a squirrel, and we still weren't desperate enough to try the dried out, month-old coyote meat hanging in the back.

As Moses continued to read love poems, I drifted off, visualizing dancing with Elizabeth's filet mignon strips rather than my past cat girlfriends.

Winnie hoped they caught a fox soon.

Thinking about foxes made her think about Mr. Cox and his cat traps again. She'd have to ask Michael at school if any other neighborhood cats went missing over winter break. Winnie was excited to have a few good reasons to return. She pulled out a sheet of paper and wrote:

Reminders:
1. Ask Ms. Green about Schallenberger's rescue and if he had books to read to help the time go by and keep him company.

2. Ask Michael if anymore cats had gone missing.
3. Ask Lucy if she wanted to be friends.
4. Find a new book in the class library since I only have one chapter left of great-great-grandma Winnifred's pioneer story.

CHAPTER THIRTEEN

Best Friends

WINNIE concluded that her last few days of winter break were the longest ever in her whole life; they had gone by so slow with all the rain, alone time, and minimal distractions that she was actually thrilled to go back to school.

Time had crawled by like a tortoise crossing the road. She couldn't *imagine* what Moses must have experienced during three long months of snowed-in isolation after only three homebound rainy days for herself. He literally must have had the most extreme case of cabin fever imaginable.

After such loneliness, Winnie went back to school a changed girl. She was determined to make friends; no more shy, quiet, "poor me" Winnifred. She woke up before her alarm and dressed with a new confidence. She glanced in the mirror and smiled while repeating her new intention, "I'm making friends today." Then she briskly walked to Schallenberger Elementary with her reminder sheet in pocket.

As Winnie approached the classroom door, Lucy bounced up and down, waving to her. Lucy was like a bundle of firecrackers ready to explode with sparkling energy.

Winnie had thought she was the most bored fourth-grader over break, but Lucy appeared to have been even more bored, especially since she missed the two weeks before with her flu and quarantine period.

Winnie gave her a wave back.

Lucy animatedly grabbed Winnie's arm and didn't stop talking until the teacher quieted everyone down. Then morning recess came, and the same thing happened: Lucy chirped sentences in Winnie's ear. Lunch came and Lucy continued incessantly talking, in between bites of sandwich, tightly holding onto Winnie's arm; then afternoon recess came and she babbled and babbled and babbled on, with

Winnie's arm still held firm; and finally at school dismissal, Lucy intertwined her arm through Winnie's while picking up the conversation where she had left off at recess. Oblivious to her surroundings because she was talking so much, Lucy walked Winnie all the way to her new house.

While Lucy rapidly chatted away, Winnie realized she hadn't even had a second to ask Michael or Ms. Green the questions about Mr. Cox or Schallenberger. And she obviously didn't need to ask Lucy about being friends.

It had just happened.

Lucy had even grabbed Winnie as a partner for the morning math activity. She hadn't looked for another partner first. She'd just gone straight to Winnie!

Winnie noticed Charley and Molly looked a bit sad not being paired with Winnie as a last pick.

Lucy walked Winnie up to her front door then gave a huge hug and said, "Thanks again for the gorgeous Get Well card. It's hanging on my bedroom wall and was my favorite one. You're a really good artist, better than that snotty Molly. Let's be best friends, okay? I have so much to tell you, and I feel like we just got started, so see you tomorrow and I will continue telling you about Aunt Betsy's awful Christmas cheesecake. It was so bad we put soy sauce on it to flavor it up. Bye, Winnie. Hey, do you want to walk to school together in the morning? I'll swing by at 7:30 a.m., and you can tell me about your break and about the gold bracelet, too. Got to go, my mom gets mad if I'm super late."

She waved and began skipping down the street toward her house.

Winnie hadn't heard half of what Lucy had said that entire day, but didn't care, she had a best friend! No more pouting, self-pitying, new-girl sorrows for Winnie. She had a best friend!

Plus, she now knew the whole respect pledge, where the Health Center was located, and how to get home. She was part of Schallenberger Elementary's fourth-grade class now. The best part was that Winnie really didn't have to change much. She remained quiet yet attentive most of the day and let Lucy fill in the rest of the spaces.

Winnie followed Lucy's lead and skipped right through her front door. Buttons greeted her with dirty paws and an eager tail wag.

"Buttons, we made it. I think I really like my new school," Winnie shared while thinking about the heroic young Moses Schallenberger and Biggs the pioneer cat making it through their heroic winter break, too. Time to find out how they were rescued, and if there were any more details about that gold cat collar bracelet.

She'd bring it to school tomorrow and tell Lucy all about great-great-grandma Winnifred's pioneer notebook story, heirloom box, and special 170-year-old gold bracelet.

CHAPTER FOURTEEN

Rescued at Last

WINNIE pulled out the heirloom box from under her bed and looked at all the contents again. She'd bravely decided that she would share the notebook and gold cat collar bracelet tomorrow during her "3 Minute Informal Oral Presentation." Ms. Green had one student a day come up to the front of the class and share, teach, demonstrate, explain anything they liked as long as it was "fourth-grade appropriate." Her teacher believed that practicing casual, informal speaking in front of others took the fear out of formal speeches.

Today, Charley had verbally walked the class through how to make a peanut butter and banana sandwich while playing video games. Winnie thought that was more "first-grade appropriate," but she wasn't surprised coming from Charley.

Winnie realized she had been so preoccupied with her new best friend, Lucy, that she hadn't had a chance to finish the last chapter in class. She opened the notebook.

It was late February, and I was beginning to recite Lord Byron's poems over and over and over in my head from delirium and dehydration. We hadn't seen Walter the Wolf in weeks, nor any foxes. Even Mrs. Squirrel wasn't out and about. I didn't have the energy to cook up some coyote meat as our last resort. So when Moses shook me and pointed at a silhouette out yonder, I thought I was seeing things, like a desert mirage or oasis, but in the snow. The manlike form kept getting closer and larger, and I had to rub my eyes with both cat paws and blink a few times before I let myself hope that someone was really approaching our log cabin.

Then the rugged bearlike figure gave a heartfelt holler, "Moses Schallenberger, it's me, Dennis Martin from Canada. I've come to save you." Moses looked at me, then looked out at the man, then at me again and began to cry. For three months, we had persevered through the coldest winter we had ever encountered.

Dennis marched right up to the cabin. "I'll be damned, you two rascals survived. You both look terrible, but you're alive. We haven't lost one pioneer from our party. Your sister is going to be overjoyed when I bring you two back."

Dennis reached in his backpack and gave us some beef jerky while rubbing Moses's shoulders to circulate blood flow. We devoured it, along with some of the best stale, smelly bread I've ever tasted.

Dennis chuckled and pointed to the eleven coyotes hanging in the back. "Guess you two weren't fond of the old coyote grub, and geez, you two are walking skeletons. Eat some more, because we're heading down the mountain in the morning and will return *for the wagons in the spring when the snow completely melts and the oxen can make the trek. Elisha Stevens, our fearless leader, told me you two were the valuables to bring back and forget about the wagons. Sorry I couldn't come sooner. It was a brutal winter, and I couldn't make the hike until some of the treacherous conditions lessened."*

Winnie suddenly realized why her great-great-grandma Winnifred showed so much interest in Schallenberger and wrote a story about him. He was the unspoken historical hero of the very first pioneer group to cross directly over to California and pave a shorter path rather than coming down from the Oregon Trail. The trouble was, the Donner Party's harrowing and dramatic experience two years later had overshadowed Schallenberger's historical significance. Several books and articles had been written about the Donner Party's deaths, starvations, and suspected cannibalism, and made Schallenberger's feat seem less important. But Winnie realized now just how important it really was. And why it mattered so much that her school was named after him!

Winnie wondered whether her great-great-grandma really had dated Moses's great-great-grandson. If so, she had an additional reason for sharing Shallenberger's traveling story. She had a human connection.

We hobbled down that mountain with our expert Canadian trapper/mountain man, Dennis, and immediately were met with hugs. Everyone from our party wanted to hear our story. Elizabeth wouldn't stop fussing over us, and groomed and fed us constantly. We slept for an entire week.

Bless her heart, Elizabeth was a good human, but unfortunately her much older husband, Dr. Townsend, was the first and only doctor in California and was treating the cholera epidemic that had reached this new territory. (Remember the bad drinking water that caused diarrhea?) He caught the darn diarrhea disease himself, then gave it to Elizabeth. They both died within two days of each other!

So I was once again Moses's mate. I secretly didn't mind, though, because by that time Moses had been practicing Lord Byron's love tips on the ladies and landed himself a real compassionate one named Fannie. They took in Elizabeth's orphaned son, John Henry Moses, and had an additional five more children themselves. Forty years after Moses's and my 1844-1845 stranded winter, he dictated the events to one of his daughters as a historic diary to share some of the facts about the journey.

Moses quietly went down in the history books, kept his very long and ugly beard, and lived until the ripe age of eighty-three, and I like to believe that I, Biggs, the wisest, bravest, most handsome, pioneer cat around, had a lot to do with his accomplishments.

So remember, next time you see a cat, pay your respects with a pat and don't be fooled— we are the guiding forces behind our human two-legged companions.

The End

Winnie spotted a folded heart shaped piece of paper at the back of the notebook. She opened it.

I dedicate this book to my loving sweetheart Moses Schallenberger III, named after his heroic great-great-grandfather. Thank you for sharing his pioneer adventure with me. I promise to pass on his courageous story to the next generations. And I will always cherish the gold cat collar bracelet you gave to me. May it, too, be passed down to historical caring souls.

Winnie gasped! Her question had been answered! Her great-great-grandma *did* know Schallenberger's great-great-grandson in high school. That's why she'd written the story.

Winnie admired the antique gold bracelet on her wrist. She would cherish this aged heirloom her whole entire life. It was a piece of California history, belonging to a completely different time period, yet it had survived several decades.

Winnie desperately wanted to believe that Biggs was with Moses throughout their winter ordeal and pioneer life, but she knew that, logically, he was probably a creation of her great-great-grandma Winnifred's—a representation of her favorite cat, as seen in the old black-and-white photo. But who knew. Maybe Biggs really did live nine cat lives. Either way, Winnie was satisfied knowing the truth and history about the gold heirloom bracelet.

She magically felt a kindred connection to her school, Schallenberger Elementary, and her great-great-grandma Winnifred, whom she was named after but had never met.

Winnie was proud and eager to share the notebook story and bracelet with her class.

CHAPTER FIFTEEN

The New Boy

ON THEIR morning walk to school, Winnie had shared all about the bracelet, her heirloom box, and the notebook story. Lucy was mystified by all the correlations and felt like the old notebook was more like a Nancy Drew mystery than a plain old story written by a grandma. Lucy was determined to play detective and figure out the missing pieces about the darn cat.

Once at school, Winnie was mentally reviewing her thoughts on great-great-grandma's story for her "3 Minute Informal Oral Presentation" for the class. She glanced at her wrist and gently rubbed the gold bracelet for good luck. Ms. Green was just about to announce Winnie as the Three Minute Speaker for the day when the classroom door opened and the principal guided a new boy into their fourth-grade room. Ms. Green nervously jumped up and fussed over her hair while telepathically glaring at the class, especially in Charley's direction, "Best behavior and no goofing off, it's your principal, and I don't want to get fired."

The principal showed off his pearly whites, then said, "Excuse me for the interruption Fourth-Grade, but Martin here just transferred from Donner Elementary in Elk Grove, California. He will be joining your class as a new student, so please make him feel welcome here at Schallenberger Elementary. It can be challenging transferring schools in the Winter. He must have some good pioneer heritage with the luck of his consecutive school names." The principal chuckled as he strolled out the door.

Winnie's mouth dropped! This kid was transferring to her school just like she had in the Fall, and moving from a school named after the Donner Party.

Pioneer history was following her everywhere!

She glared in Martin's direction and suddenly realized she actually liked being the only new student in her fourth-grade class. She didn't want another one. And what about poor Schallenberger, always overshadowed by the darn Donner Party's harrowing legacy? Winnie was proud that her school was named after Schallenberger, the neglected hero, and that she had a special connection to him through her great-great-grandma's notebook and bracelet.

Now Winnie had learned that the Donner Party had a school named after one of their members, too. Poor Moses?

And what about the lake Biggs and Schallenberger trapped foxes by! It had been renamed from Truckee Lake to Donner Lake just two years after their experience to honor the Donner Party's defeating, ill-fated winter stay.

Winnie felt a bit guilty for such negative thoughts, especially since only forty-five of the original eighty-one Donner members had survived, but she felt like her Schallenberger was being overlooked once again.

Martin, the new kid, remained standing in the front of the class with hands in pockets; he jerked his head to one side, flipping strands of hair out of his eyes then looked around.

Ms. Green cleared her throat while recovering from the unexpected new addition and shuffled a desk together next to Winnie's. "Martin, is there anything you'd like to share with the class about your old school while I get you some school supplies and find you a chair?"

"Sure, well first, how do you say this school name and who is this Scall-uhhh-hamburger guy?"

The class laughed.

Charley loudly interjected, "He was a pioneer who ate a lot of beef jerky."

Martin nodded his head. "My last school was named after a famous pioneer, too, much easier to pronounce. Donner Elementary, you know after the legendary Donner Party that took the short-cut through the Sierra Nevada Mountains and got stuck for five months and had to eat one another to survive." He paused to measure the shocked and horrific expressions.

Winnie mentally corrected him. *Moses Schallenberger was the first to pave that shortcut, your party came afterward, and that's called cannibalism, eating one's own species!*

Molly, Ms. Know-It-All, nodded approvingly in Martin's direction as he continued, "Well my school was named after the party leader, George Donner's daughter, Elitha Donner, she was only fourteen when they were rescued." He stopped again to check for surprised responses, then carried on, "and one of the dudes who rescued her from Sutter's Fort in 1847 asked her to marry him a month later, and she did!!"

The class was in an uproar with moans of disgust and disbelief.

Charley shouted, "She got married at fourteen, isn't that illegal? That would be like my eighth-grade brother who can't work the microwave without blowing something up getting married. No one would even step foot in his stinky room, yuck."

Winnie gagged at the thought of getting married in four years.

Ms. Green hustled back to the front of the classroom and kindly ushered Martin back to his new seat. "Quiet down class, thank you Martin for the history lesson. Schallenberger could easily have been a friend of Elitha Donner."

She opened his social studies book to page ninety-one. "Here is a paragraph about Moses Schallenberger, who was stranded in the same exact place as Elitha just two years before."

Now it was Martin's turn to be surprised. He examined the historical black-and-white photo of the old man with a long, scraggly beard.

Ms. Green walked back to the front of the room. "Today's 3 Minute Informal Speaker is Winnie."

Winnie glanced at Lucy, who gave her an encouraging thumbs up.

Winnie took a deep breath then began to share with the rest of her classmates about the story. She even included the romantic connection between her great-great-grandma Winnifred and Schallenberger's great-great-grandson.

Ms. Green was on the edge of her seat and completely lost track of the 3 minute time limit. And almost every hand shot up for questions about Biggs, the coyotes, the Christmas coffee, and Walter the Wolf—information not included in the one paragraph in their social studies books.

Molly confidently stated, "Winnie your great-great-grandma was an expert historian on Moses Schallenberger. You may need to share her notebook with the San Jose Historical Society. And if I'm doing my calculations correct, the timeframe works for your great-great-grandma being the same age as Moses's great-great-grandson."

Only Molly would think to fact-check the age timeline of the story, thought Winnie.

Charley hollered, "I get it now. You have that funny old name after your great-great-grandma. Hey, are you related to Schallenberger somehow? Are you famous, Winnie?"

Winnie's cheeks flushed as she shook her head no.

Michael raised his hand. "Winnie, do you know what happened to the gold cat collar bracelet you told us about?"

Winnie had almost forgotten the grand finale! She held up her wrist and let the shiny gold shimmer in the sunlight from the window. Everyone oohed and ahhed.

Charley spoke again. "Winnie I think this is the best 3 Minute Informal Oral Presentation we've ever had, especially since you've gone over thirty minutes into math time."

Charley hated math. He continued, "Ms. Green, can Winnie be the surprise speaker again tomorrow?"

Winnie blushed and headed back to her seat. She was so touched to be a part of this group now.

Martin, the new kid smiled at her and quietly whispered, "Wow that was some story about Biggs and Moses. Could I maybe read it some time?"

Winnie unconsciously flashed back to Chapter Twelve of *Biggs, the Pioneer Cat* about Lord Byron's romantic love poems and double blushed as her heart skipped a beat.

The End

Fun Facts

1. This book is historical fiction: a story that is made up but set in the past and sometimes borrows true characteristics of the time period.
2. Moses Schallenberger was a real person who traveled with the Stephens-Townsend-Murphy Party and was rescued by Canadian trapper Dennis Martin. He had a sister Elizabeth, married to Dr. Townsend, who both died within two days of each other.
3. Biggs is a real-live cat who belongs to the author's sister and nephew, but was a fictional character in the journey across

the Sierra Nevada Mountains, even though
some pioneer women did attempt to bring
their pet cats.

4. Schallenberger was stranded 1844–1845
   winter and dictated his experience to
   one of his daughters forty years later.
   He listed reading the two books—Lord
   Byron's poems and Lord Chesterfield's
   social etiquette letters—to his son. Most
   likely there was a Bible, too, but he did
   not mention this in his journal. He did
   use pine knots in the fire as a nighttime
   reading light.

5. It has been strongly suggested and passed
   on as folklore that the Donner Party practiced
   cannibalism during their stranded winter,
   however historians found no human bones
   around the lake site. Donner Memorial
   State Park Museum is located right next
   to Donner Lake and the Truckee River.

6. There is a twenty-two-foot tall pioneer
   monument by the Visitors' Center, at the
   Donner Memorial State Park close to the
   location where Moses Schallenberger's cabin
   stood. It is California Historical Landmark

#134. The height represents the snow depth during the Donner Party's winter of 1846–1847.

7. Sutter's Fort is now a State Park Museum in Sacramento California

8. Elitha Donner was rescued and married a month after at Sutter Fort at the age of fourteen; there was a shortage of wives, and a school was named after her where she is buried in Elk Grove, Sacramento.

9. Moses did live off the two dead cows and their dried meat and used it to bait foxes into the traps.

10. George R. Stewart was an expert historian, author, and English professor at the University of California, Berkeley and wrote a book, *The Pioneers Go West* and several articles about the Stevens-Townshend-Murphy Party using facts from Moses's journey manuscript, which was reproduced by Horace S. Foote in his history of San Jose called Pen Pictures.

11. Moses did celebrate Christmas Day with one cup of coffee.

12. Moses Schallenberger was found with eleven coyotes hanging behind his log cabin and

stated in his journal that the flavor was
disgusting compared to fox.

13. Schallenberger Elementary School is located
in San Jose, California, and the author really
did transfer midyear.

14. Elizabeth, Dr. Townsend, and Moses's parents
all died from cholera, which is almost extinct
in the U.S. today.

15. Moses Schallenberger lived until the ripe age
of eighty-three and had five children, plus his
sister's orphaned son, with his wife Fannie.
He is buried in Oak Hill Memorial Park,
Pioneer section in San Jose, California.

16. Cats, on average, live longer than dogs.

MOSES SCHALLENBERGER